WOLF HUNT

WOLF HUNT

In a rusty tin hut near Bletchley a group of Oxford dons pored over the latest coded message from Enigma, the newly captured German cipher machine. The message stated that the Grey Wolf was once again on the move. From that cryptic but startling intelligence, Force Ultra was born – a group of men so daring and so secret that only the elite in British Intelligence were sure of their existence. Men whose first mission was to infiltrate the heart of Nazi Germany, hunt out the lair of the man they called Grey Wolf, and then kill him...

WOLF HUNT

by

Charles Whiting

Dales Large Print Books
Long Preston, North Yorkshire,
BD23 4ND, England.

British Library Cataloguing in Publication Data.

Whiting, Charles
    Wolf hunt.

    A catalogue record of this book is
    available from the British Library

    ISBN   1-84262-434-2 pbk

First published in Great Britain in 1976 by
Futura Publications Limited

Copyright © Charles Whiting 1976

Cover illustration © André Leonard by arrangement with
P.W.A. International Ltd.

The moral right of the author has been asserted

Published in Large Print 2006 by arrangement with
Eskdale Publishing Ltd.

Dales Large Print is an imprint of Library Magna Books Ltd.

Printed and bound in Great Britain by
T.J. (International) Ltd., Cornwall, PL28 8RW

'The Battle for Europe will not be won by some daring secret agent in the backstreets of Lyons or Metz. It will be won here at Bletchley by a bunch of elderly Oxford dons working in a rusty tin hut in the middle of the home counties.'

Zero C, of the Secret Intelligence Service to Major Cain, Summer 1942.

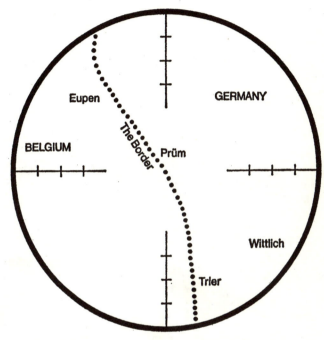

A MISSION IS PROPOSED (July 1942)

ONE

Major Cain could see that the Heinkel was going to attempt a crash landing. It was coming in low over the flat dawn Buckinghamshire countryside with a thick plume of black smoke pouring from its shell-damaged port engine and little scarlet tongues of flame licking at the cowling. The fear-crazed pilot attempted to wrestle the undercarriage down as he throttled back his speed in order to land.

Cain changed gear with his steel hook, and brought his camouflaged staff car to a halt on the narrow road which ran to Bletchley. He guessed that the stricken Heinkel was heading for the forty-acre grass field to the right of the road, and if the pilot couldn't make it, he did not want to be at the receiving end of twenty tons of German bomber.

The Heinkel's second engine was beginning to cough and splutter alarmingly now. Cain shrugged slightly, his dark face expressionless. After three years of the toughest kind of combat against the Germans, he felt no sympathy for the unknown Jerry pilot struggling so desperately to bring his stricken plane down.

The Heinkel was flying just above the tops of the great oaks ahead of him. Cain could see its black and white cross quite plainly and the pale blur of the pilot's contorted face behind the spider web of cracked Perspex. The starboard engine gave one last asthmatic cough and failed. In the sudden silence the plane hissed down to its destruction, clearing the road and scattering a shower of leaves behind it. The port wing dipped. It caught the ground and snapped like matchwood. The plane swung round, swaying and shuddering madly, and at 100 miles an hour crashed nose-first into one of the great oaks.

For a moment there was an echoing silence. Then Cain rammed home first awkwardly with his new hook. The little staff car rattled forward. Something was beginning to stir in the crashed bomber. With his free hand, Cain fumbled for his pistol. Even in the comparative safety of the Home Counties he was never without it.

But Major Cain was not destined to reach the German plane first. Just as the sirens started to sound the 'all clear' over at Bletchley, two Bren gun carriers swung round the bend in the road. In the first one, the officer in Home Guard uniform, standing upright next to the radio operator, took in the situation at a glance. He waved to the second carrier to stop Cain's car, then rapped an

12

order to his own driver. The driver swung the carrier off the road. It crashed through the hedge, and at twenty miles an hour rattled over the uneven ground towards the plane.

Meanwhile the second carrier skidded to a halt and slewed round, blocking the road. As Cain braked, the Home Guard sergeant in command brought up his Bren gun; there was no mistaking the look on his face: he would not hesitate to use it if Cain failed to stop. Cain applied the brake and opened the door.

'What the hell's going on here, Sergeant,' he began. 'Have you gone out of–'

The rattle of machine-gun fire interrupted his words.

Cain spun round. The first carrier had come to a stop, fifty yards away from the plane. Crouched over the Bren, the Home Guard officer was systematically spraying the whole length of the Heinkel. Slowly the door of the Heinkel started to open. The Home Guard officer immediately swung his weapon round. A hand clawed desperately at the metal. The Home Guard squeezed the trigger again. The butt kicked back and the Bren shuddered violently. Tracer cut through the air. Lead stitched a pattern around the hand. Slowly the hand started to slide down the length of the door, dragging a trail of blood behind it. Only then did the officer take his finger off the trigger.

'What the devil are you fellows up to?' Cain demanded of the Home Guard Captain. 'It's the Home Guard's job to take Jerry air crew prisoners and hold them till the Regular Army arrives – not to shoot the poor bastards.' He nodded at the silent plane and its dead crew.

The Home Guard Captain, who was in his mid-twenties and looked like a highly-trained professional soldier, did not even flush. 'Can you identify yourself, Major?' he rapped and held out his hand, while his men covered Cain with their weapons.

Cain's lean face tensed angrily. But he knew there was no point in arguing with these men; he had just witnessed how ruthless they could be. With his hook, he opened his pocket and took out his pass.

The Home Guard Captain scanned it quickly. 'SOE, eh, Major?'

The Home Guard's hard, suspicious eyes took in Cain's face, the steel hook, the new ribbons of the MC and the DSO on his chest.

'Can I ask what a member of the Special Operations Executive is doing in this neck of the woods at this time of the day, Major?'

'I have been asked to report to something called the Government Code and Cypher School over there at Bletchley. I've answered your question, Captain. Now you can answer

14

mine – who the hell are you and what kind of unit is this anyway?' With an angry wave of his hook, Cain indicated the men still circling the lane. 'What kind of killers are they?'

'*I'll* tell you, Major Cain!'

Cain spun round. He had not heard the civilian walking across the field. For such a tall man he had moved with surprising lightness and speed. The man gave him a brief smile, but his blue eyes did not light up. The Home Guard Captain standing next to Cain stiffened to attention. The civilian nodded to him to stand at ease and said:

'You wanted to know who those killers are, Major Cain? I'll tell you. You've just met Ultra security from something called the Government Code and Cypher School.'

TWO

Zero C broke his silence for the first time as they parked the car and started walking up the drive towards the large ornate red brick house with its timbered gables.

'The Government Code and Cypher School, or as we in the Old Firm call it "the Golf and Chess Club". Most of them are from the older universities, dons and the like, though we have a couple of musicians and naturally several chess and crossword maestros.'

Major Cain wondered about the 'naturally'. Nothing seemed natural about this strange organisation with its innocuous name, guarded by a bunch of ruthless killers and staffed apparently by a group of fusty old professors who relaxed in the middle of total war on the golf links or over their chess boards. And what was he to make of this strange civilian, who had introduced himself as 'Zero C' and was obviously a big noise in the Secret Intelligence Service? But in the last three years of his clandestine work, Major Cain had learned to control his curiosity. So he said nothing, but kept his eyes open as Zero C guided him to a small collection of nissen huts signposted with the brutal warning:

WD PROPERTY –
TRESPASSERS WILL BE SHOT

'Home,' Zero C said, halting outside Hut Number Three. He knocked on the door.

It was opened immediately, as if the Home Guardsman, tommy gun slung over his shoulder, had been following their progress all the time from the gate. With a grunt, he examined their passes and allowed them to enter.

'What have you got in here?' asked Major

Cain, 'the ruddy crown jewels!'

Zero C gave the SOE Major another of his wintry smiles. 'Yes, something like that. But please sit down, Major.' He indicated the young men in the uniforms of all three services bent over paperwork around the overheated, airless hut. 'Don't worry about my boys. Here we can speak quite openly.'

'About what? To be frank, I'm almost speechless.'

'I understand. It must be all very bewildering for you, Major. That nasty business with the Hun bomber, the Home Guard chaps – most of them come from Welsh Guards by the way – and the security at this place – all to protect a bunch of elderly Oxford dons apparently working in some routine government training school. But as you'll learn very soon, we can't be too careful about our security at Bletchley. That's why we had to take care of that unfortunate bomber crew. The Heinkel flew over here twice just after dawn. And we had to make sure that if any of the crew *had* seen anything, they didn't go blabbing about it once they were in the cage with the rest of their Hun compatriots. It wouldn't be the first time that a group of POWs built an illegal transmitter. We did in the First War.' He chuckled softly at a private memory.

Cain looked curiously at the tall, sharp-featured civilian with the blond hair now going grey, wondering who he really was and why he, an experienced SOE officer with three years' secret combat behind him, should have been posted to this strange organisation.

Zero C seemed to be able to read the younger man's mind. 'Now I suppose you're wondering, Cain, why you have been posted here by Baker Street eh? I mean with your record, I am sure you thought that Brigadier Gubbins would have sent you back to the Continent, once your hand had healed.'

'The thought had crossed my mind. Our organisation in Europe desperately needs every man it can get, if we're ever going to beat the Jerries.'

'There you are wrong, my dear Major,' Zero C said easily. 'The battle for Europe will not be won by some daring secret agent in the backstreets of Lyons or Metz. It will be won here at Bletchley by a bunch of elderly Oxford dons working in a rusty tin hut in the middle of the home counties. And that Major Cain is why you have been posted here. You see this place is a cover for the Ultra Organisation, which one day, God willing, will win the war for this country. Here at Bletchley our tame experts break every German message, from those sent by divisions, right up to those dispatched by Hitler himself.'

'You mean—'

'Yes, I mean that we can read all the messages sent by the German armed forces almost as quickly as their German recipients can and we have been able to do so for nearly two years now. You see, Major, we in the Old Firm had a tremendous stroke of luck. We managed to lay our greedy hands on a copy of the German Enigma.'

'The what?'

'The top secret German coding machine which since 1939 has been used to encode all high-level German military and political communications. We'd guessed before the war that the Huns would attempt to use some mechanical system of encoding their messages to replace the old one-pad method of coding. When we heard from Polish Intelligence in the summer of thirty-nine that one of their people in Germany had been employed in a Hun factory where they were making a coding machine named the Enigma on a large scale, we knew that the Huns had pulled it off. One month later we had a complete Enigma in our hands. In essence it is based on a system of changing the words in the message by progressive proliferation so that the recipient who has the key to the system can set his own machine and thus quickly unscramble the message into clear. So far so good. But back here our experts worked out that it would take a team of the top mathematical brains in the country a whole month to work out the key to a single cipher setting.

'I am no technical expert so I cannot explain how our experts did it. But working like hell down here with the aid of some of the finest brains in the country, they came up with another machine which could unscramble the Enigma key-settings. We call it the Oracle of Bletchley. It looks like a bronze-coloured Eastern Goddess. And since the spring of 1940, that particular Oracle has revealed to us every enemy military and diplomatic secret.'

For a moment, Major Cain was too shocked to speak. Then he blurted out. 'But if that is the case and we're getting that kind of information in advance, why are we in the mess we are in? After three years of war, the Jerries dominate most of Europe and we've been chased out of one country after another. Hell, we haven't had one single victory!'

Zero C held up his hands as if he wished to ward off a blow. 'I know, I know, Major. You would have thought that with our prior knowledge of where and when and how the enemy will strike, we would have a trump card up our sleeves. But you don't know our senior commanders. When we pass on our information – naturally we don't divulge to them what its source is – some of them don't really believe it or don't take it seriously enough. Last year in Crete for instance, we warned the commander there that the Germans were going to launch an airborne attack. But the general in question didn't take our warning with due seriousness.' He shrugged. 'So what happened? We had to pick up our bags and run for it once again. But that's only part of our problem, Cain. There is another aspect.' His voice rose again. 'You see, when our Oracle reads the Enigma's messages, we are sometimes forced to sit on our thumbs and wait for the Hun to begin his operations. There is simply nothing we can do to hamper the Hun's intentions. But if for instance, last year when the Huns were planning their operations at the Hotel Grande Bretagne in Athens, which we knew all about – thanks to the Oracle – we could have taken out all their senior paratroop commanders – Student, von der Heydte, Meindl and so on – we could have set back their operations for weeks. We might well have been able to have it postponed altogether. You understand what I mean?'

Cain's eyes lit up. 'Of course!' he exclaimed. 'If our senior commanders are too slow or too ill-prepared to make full use of the information you get from this Enigma thing, the problem could be taken right out of their hands by killing the expert or the irreplaceable senior commander, rather like the Colonel Keyes' attempt to knock out

Field Marshal Rommel in Africa last year. Why, it could add a completely new dimension to clandestine warfare. Instead of the bludgeon we've been using in SOE and commando operations these last two years, with the help of that machine of yours, we could start wielding a stiletto.'

Zero C smiled. 'I was hoping that you would react in the way you've just done, Cain when I asked the PM for permission to have SOE transfer you to my organisation – Ultra.'

'You mean Churchill was involved?' Cain asked incredulously.

Zero C nodded. 'Yes. You see this unit has such a high security rating (that is why we had to find a completely new rating for it, Ultra Secret) that the PM has to approve personally everybody who is to be let into the secret. And with your record in front of him,' he looked down at the dossier on the desk, 'it didn't take him too long to give his approval.' For a moment, he flipped open the cover and stared down at it.

'Sandhurst 1935 – Sword of Honour,' he read thoughtfully.

'With Wingate on clandestine ops in Palestine a year later. Transferred to Le Grand's D for Destruction Department of my own organisation in thirty-nine. Attempted to blow up the Iron Gates on the Danube in forty–'

'And failed,' Cain interjected.

'But you didn't fail in Rotterdam in forty when you won your MC,' Zero C said easily. 'Or in France when you ran the Comet Network for the SOE last year, though you had to pay a high price for it,' he nodded at Cain's right hook, which replaced the hand blown off when the SS had raided the Maquisards' hideout in the forest.

Cain shrugged. 'It's a tough war over there, sir, and anyone who goes into it must expect to pay the price.' His voice rose. 'But at all events it's better than wearing out the seat of one's pants in some office-bound job in London.'

Zero C accepted the bait. 'Well, I can assure you that you are not going to be office-bound here at Bletchley. Ultra has plans for you. Major Cain I am authorised to offer you the command of the new Ultra Force, which will put this organisation on the offensive at last.'

'I accept,' Cain said hurriedly. 'But what is this new force?'

Zero C tugged the end of his sharp nose. 'At this moment it does not exist. It will be up to you to recruit it, Major Cain. And you will have exactly one week to do so.' He opened a drawer and slid a sealed envelope across the desk to Cain. 'In that envelope you'll find the names and personal details of the men the Old Firm feels will be most suitable for your new unit. Naturally they will be told nothing of what is really happening here at Bletchley. All they will be told is that they are to belong to a special operational unit named Ultra – no more. Do you understand, Major?'

'Yes. But one week seems to be very little time to get a special force together.'

'I know. But time is of the essence. You see, Major, we've got a mission for Ultra.'

THREE

Major Cain walked slowly down from the sombre Scottish manor house that was the home of Special Training School No 1, towards the training area next to the sea loch. It was raining – a thin bitter Highland drizzle – and the loch was wrapped in mist. Cain shuddered. Everything here seemed grey: the house behind him, the loch, the very heather which stretched to a grey forbidding horizon.

But there was nothing grey about the men in the uniforms of half a dozen Allied armies spread out in small training groups all over the moorland. Here the predominant colour was crimson – the crimson of sweating, strained faces as the SOE instructors put the new recruits through their paces, doubling them through the soaked heather with sixty-pound packs on their backs.

Cain stopped for a moment and looked around for the American uniform he was looking for. Then he spotted it, one of a group of six men around a tall, spare instructor with steel-rimmed glasses. That would be his man – Captain Alfred Abel, US Army, seconded to the new secret OSS organisation. For a moment Cain paused and stared down at the card Zero C had given him.

'*Abel*, Alfred b. 1919. American. Educ Exeter College, Princeton. Instructor Mod. Langs. Cornell 1932. Asst. Prof. College Park. U of Maryland 1936. Volunteered for Abraham Lincoln Battn, International Brigade, 1937. Service in Spain 1937–39. Joined US Counter-Intelligence Corps 1941, transferred with the rank of Captain to the OSS 1942.'

Thoughtfully he put the card back into his pocket with the aid of his hook and stared at the tall blond American listening attentively to his instructor. A college professor who had volunteered to fight against Franco in Spain during the Civil War? Did that make the man a Communist perhaps. If he were, that wouldn't be too good. He had experienced the Communists in France with the Maquis. They were touchy and decidedly uncooperative, fighting their own kind of war against

25

the Germans. Or worse – was he perhaps one of those American idealists, like the American professor in Hemingway's new book on the Spanish Civil War? He had met enough of them in London since he had returned to duty after his wound. With their idealistic enthusiasm, they could turn out to be a positive danger once they were sent out into the field.

Cain sniffed and continued his progress towards the attentive group of students listening to their instructor, who despite his benign appearance, was STS's unarmed combat man.

'You see, gentlemen, your aim in unarmed combat is not to kill the Jerry,' he was saying. 'No, your aim is to put him in dock for six months. You see a wounded Jerry is more bother to his own people live than dead. A wounded soldier has to be looked after, wasting Jerry manpower. A dead soldier is buried and forgotten.'

Cain flashed a glance at the American. His frank features showed obvious disgust at the instructor's brutal words. Nevertheless, Cain noted the determination stamped on the American Captain's face; he had seen that kind of determination before in men who fought on when tougher men had already given up, hanging on grimly like a terrier on to its enemy and only relaxing its hold in the moment of death. He wiped the raindrops from his face and waited.

'Now most of you will be armed with a knife,' the instructor continued. 'But don't rely on it. A swift kick in the ballocks will be just as effective.' He grinned, revealing that all his front teeth were missing. 'Now then, you Novak, come at me with your knife and I'll show you what I mean.'

Novak, a squat Pole, did not need a second invitation. He pushed at the instructor, knife raised. The bespectacled instructor waited calmly. With surprising speed his left arm hissed upwards, as if it were worked by a steel spring. The knife went flying from Novak's hand. The instructor's boot flashed upwards and caught the Pole in the crotch. It was not a hard kick, but it was hard enough to send Novak flying into the wet heather, his broad face contorted with agony, his hands grasping frantically for his injured testicles.

The instructor grinned. 'I must be a bit more careful with my big feet, gentlemen, mustn't I? But you see what I mean by a good swift kick in the ballocks?'

Abel bent down and helped the Pole and then turned to the grinning instructor, his thin, freckled face tense with rage. 'That was sheer brutality.'

'Yes,' the instructor said easily. 'But it will teach you all a lesson. Never trust anybody. And where you lot are going, that lesson may save your lives one day.'

Cain nodded approvingly. The instructor was right. There was no time for false concepts of morality and decency in the kind of fighting these trainees would engage in; in their world it would be dog eat dog.

'Do you mind then, if I have a go with the knife?' Abel asked, his voice full of barely contained menace.

'Certainly. Now you know what to expect, you'll probably do a better job than Novak there.'

Abel said nothing. Bending, he picked up the knife. Instead of raising it above his head as the Pole had done, he pressed the wicked blade tightly to his side, waving it from side to side as he advanced slowly on the waiting instructor, left arm raised slightly to ward off any sudden move by his silent opponent.

Cain tensed. He could see from the look on the instructor's face that he was the born killer. His eyes were fixed on Abel's eyes, not on the knife, knowing that they would signal the American's move an instant before he made it. Cain held his breath and recognised the signal in the same moment that the instructor did.

Abel lunged forward. Instantly the instructor swung to one side. Abel stumbled. The instructor grabbed him by the arm. Abel shouted with pain as the other man exerted pressure and sent him flying through the air to land on his back in the wet heather.

'Lesson number two,' the instructor said calmly, without a second look at the American lying gasping on his back. 'Always expect the unexpected.'

Cain waited for the American's reaction. Would he give up now? That hold must have paralysed his right arm and the fall he had just experienced would not have helped his insides very much.

'You see, gentlemen,' the instructor continued, 'you cannot hope that your enemy—'

'*You*, I want another go,' Abel's voice cut into the instructor's words.

The bespectacled instructor turned round slowly and looked at the American as if he had just crawled out of the woodwork. 'I see,' he said carefully and bent down to pick up the knife. 'Do you want this?'

Abel shook his head. 'No, otherwise I might be tempted to plunge it into your black heart. *Now!*' He rushed forward unexpectedly, head tucked into his shoulders like an American football player.

Again the instructor reacted quicker. His right hand shot out, palm upwards and bent back slightly. It caught the American just under the nose. In one and the same instant the instructor hooked his two first fingers inside Abel's nostrils and jerked upwards.

'Lesson number three,' the instructor said softly, not even breathing hard, '*never* lose your temper. It will only let you down and make you do foolish things that you will live to regret – that is if you are lucky enough to live.'

Major Cain knew it was time to step in. The training session was getting out of hand and he wanted Abel in one piece. 'All right, sergeant,' he snapped, 'that's enough. I think you'd better dismiss your class for the day.'

The instructor turned, startled, and it was at that moment that Abel ran forward. With one bloody hand he pushed Cain so that he stumbled into the instructor. With the other he caught the man a stinging blow across the face which sent his glasses flying to the heather. Abel didn't hesitate. As Cain tried to keep his balance and failed, he jammed his heel down hard on the glasses. 'Always expect the unexpected,' he grunted and in the same instant brought his right hand up into the instructor's face.

The unarmed combat instructor shot backwards and sprawled full length in the wet heather next to a suddenly grinning Major Cain, who knew now that Captain Alfred Abel, ex-Professor of Modern Languages, was just the man he was looking for.

FOUR

'All right, you bunch of pregnant penguins,' roared the harsh voice down below on the parade ground, 'let's have them arms up now! Come on, swing 'em, left … right, left … right!... Move them legs, you 'orrible idle man you! Nothing but yer goolies will fall out… Bags of swank there now, you're on parade remember!'

The elegant, elderly commandant of Number Two Region Military Prison turned and faced the two visitors who were watching the scene at the window with him.

'They come here military criminals, gentlemen – desertion, theft, insubordination and the like – and after eighty-four days we send them back to their units as soldiers. And how do we do it?' He stroked his thin moustache, which looked as if he pencilled it on every morning after shaving. 'Not with any of this namby-pamby psychological stuff. No, we use the simplest method of all, good old British Army drill, and then more drill.' He glared at the two younger officers, as if he expected them to challenge his statement.

But both of them remained silent, staring down at the sweating shaven-headed pris-

31

oners down below being chased back and forth at the quickstep under the gimlet eyes of the immaculate 'staffs', swagger canes clamped under their right arms as if they were glued permanently there.

'Which is Brooks then?' Cain asked finally, not attempting to conceal his contempt of the elderly Major with his absurd moustache and Territorial Decoration, the only evidence of the military prowess of this man who knew how to make soldiers.

'You mean Captain, the Count Brooks – as the London dailies called him last year when the Redcaps finally caught up with him?'

Cain flashed Abel a look, and the American smiled at the sudden discomfiture of this remote British officer who had rescued him from the unthinking brutality of STS Number One two days before. Major Cain, CO of the new Ultra outfit – whatever that might be – was not a man to tolerate fools gladly. 'No, I don't mean Captain, the Count Brooks, I mean *Private* Brooks, formerly of the Special Operations Executive, serving one year here for absconding with SOE funds he was ordered to convey as a courier to France for the Maquis.'

The commandant flushed and raised his hand nervously again to his moustache, as if to reassure himself that it was still there. 'That's Brooks, down there in the squad being drilled by the RSM.'

'Ah, yes,' said Cain slowly, 'then would you be kind enough to get yourself down on to that parade ground and bring Brooks up here. I want to talk to him immediately.'

'Well, there's the beggar, Abel,' Cain said when the Commandant had gone. 'I recognise him from the photo in his dossier.'

Abel followed the direction of Cain's gaze. He saw a small, dark soldier, who, despite the fact that the black-jawed RSM was doubling his squad of prisoners back and forth on the square as if they would never stop again, seemed cool and collected.

'He looks a pretty cool customer, Major,' Abel remarked. 'I don't think anything would faze him easily.'

'He is and it wouldn't,' Cain replied. 'Brooks is a Cockney by birth and what we call in England a wide boy by inclination.' He turned to face Abel. 'According to his dossier, he started out as a barrow boy. In the mid-thirties he formed what he called the Jewish Protection League in the East End when Mosley's Blackshirts started getting tough, although he hasn't one drop of Jewish blood in him. About that time he came to the notice of several rich Jewish businessmen in the City – God knows how, but he did. They sent him out to Germany under the cover of being a rep for a Leeds textile business. He was supposed to be selling woollens to the big Rhineland chain stores. Mostly the stores had been in Jewish hands until the Nazis had forced their owners to sell at absurdly low prices to "Aryans". But there were still enough Jewish employees working in them to help Brooks with his mission.'

'Which was?'

'To smuggle out important Jews or those whose lives were most urgently threatened by the Nazis. So by early 1938 friend Brooks, the ex-Cockney barrow boy, had established a pretty effective escape route from the Rhineland via the Eifel–Ardennes into Belgium. There the Jewish Hagannah organisation took over and moved the escapees illegally into Palestine, where they could provide an additional headache for the British Mandate authorities. I should know – I was there at the time, at the receiving end of it.'

Abel whistled softly, his frank, open face clearly expressing his admiration. 'Some guy eh?'

'No. Brooks is simply a wide boy with an eye to the main chance. He was in the business for the money, nothing else. Anyway he stuck it out till 1939 when he just managed to get out of the Reich in time, with the Gestapo hot on his heels. But somebody in Military Intelligence must have heard of him and in 1940, after he had deserted from the RAF twice, he was – er – convinced that if he didn't want to do a long stretch in the

Scrubs, he'd better volunteer for the SOE. Naturally he volunteered. And he did surprisingly well. He won the Military Medal for an op he did in Belgium. His second mission and third, both in Holland, went off equally well and he was mentioned in dispatches. But on his fourth mission some fool in Baker Street made him a courier, taking two thousand pounds in gold to the Dutch Underground. It was a fatal mistake. Friend Brooks went through the standard procedures right up to Tempsford. He even got into the Lysander which was going to take him to Holland. At the very last moment he said he had to get out to take a leak. His conducting officer thought that was pretty natural. Everybody's a bit nervous at the start of a new op, and last minute nerves usually play hell with one's outside plumbing. So Brooks was allowed to get out to have a leak. The leak lasted nearly seven months until finally the Redcaps nabbed Brooks outside the Savoy. The tame Captain Count had just dined royally off black market steak and champagne. Of course the gold was gone, but in the meantime our friend had developed a stable of girls who were working the West End and was living off the money they earned on their backs. That's when the cheap dailies started calling him the Super Spiv.'

'A character eh, Major?'

'You can say that again, Abel. Our Spiv needs a very large eye kept upon him at all times because–'

'Someone taking my name in vain?' interrupted an amused Cockney voice.

Cain and Abel swung round.

An undersized soldier in an immaculate uniform, decorated with the blue wings of a man who had completed three combat jumps and the red and white ribbon of the Military Medal, stood there, his face set in a characteristic knowing, cheeky grin. Behind him the huge, black-jowled RSM gripped his brass-bound pacing stick in his hand, as if he were preparing to bring it down on the smaller man's head.

'Don't you ever knock?' Cain asked coldly.

'Yessir,' the prisoner answered. 'But you listen first, *then* you knock. Usually you can do yerself a bit of good that way, I've always found.'

'All right, come on in and close the door behind you. Sarnt-Major,' he addressed the NCO, 'you stay there and guard the door.'

The black-jowled RSM hesitated. 'Don't you want me to watch him sir?' he barked. 'He's a tricky little bugger. Give him yer little finger and he'll take the whole bloody hand – if you'll forgive me French.'

Cain's hook slapped against his pistol. 'Don't worry, Sarnt-Major, I'll take care of our friend if it's necessary.'

Cain waited till the prisoner had closed the door, then he introduced himself and the American. 'I'm Cain and this officer is Captain Abel of the US Army.'

Brooks looked at the two of them in disbelief, cocking his head to one side. 'Cain and Abel,' he echoed, 'like in the Bible? Go on, sir, you must be having me on!'

Abel laughed; he was beginning to like the little Cockney. 'Very smart, soldier,' he said. 'But we haven't come to that state of affairs yet.' He threw Cain a sidelong glance. 'Though you never know, we might do one day.'

Cain silenced him with a look. 'Brooks,' he said, 'I've got a proposition to make to you.'

The little man's grey eyes grew wary. 'What kind of proposition, sir?'

'Well Brooks—'

'Call me Spiv, it sounds more friendly – and I have a funny feeling that I'm gonna need all the friendship I can get.'

'All right, er – Spiv, this is the situation...' Swiftly, Major Cain explained the details of the new unit, ending with the words, 'so you see, Spiv, I need three specialists for a start. Captain Abel, who is OSS trained, has had combat experience and is my linguist, an explosives expert who I hope to recruit tomorrow, and you.'

'And what is my speciality supposed to be, sir?'

'You know the German borders with Holland, Belgium and Luxembourg like the back of your hand and all the smuggling routes through the Eifel and Ardennes. That's pretty useful knowledge to have.'

For what seemed a long time, the little Cockney did not answer, and the two officers observed him attentively. Outside, one of the Staffs was crying in a hoarse, beer-thickened voice. 'And when I tell you shower to get fell in on parade, I mean *get fell in!* ... I want you to come on to this square as if old Adolf himself was after yer with a ruddy flame-thrower. *Now, get fell in!*'

Slowly Spiv opened his mouth. 'Go on, Major,' he said, 'pull the other leg, will yer – it's got bells on it.'

'What do you mean?' Cain snapped.

'Well, sir, it stands to reason. There's already the SOE and the Yankees' OSS and half a dozen other private armies – sometimes it seems to me that you officers spend all yer time trying to think up new excuses for private armies – but no matter. What I'm trying to say, sir, is this. What kind of mob is this Ultra lot of yours gonna be, if it needs a linguist, an explosives expert and a bloke like me who knows the borders of the Fatherland?' He licked his lips apprehensively. 'What are we supposed to do, eh – blow up Cologne's Hohenzollern Bridge, eh or the Jerry HQ at Koblenz?'

Abel turned to Cain. 'Yeah, Spiv here is right, Major. What kind of mission could they give to Ultra that couldn't be carried out by SOE or OSS?'

Cain's dark face hardened. The two harsh lines at the sides of his mouth deepened. 'I'm not prepared to discuss the reason for Ultra's formation with either of you. Nor will I be able to do so in the future – *ever*. You both better understand that right from the start.' He turned to the prisoner once more. 'Now Spiv, I need you for Ultra. Are you prepared to volunteer for it?'

The Cockney looked at him calculatingly. 'What's in it for me, Major?'

'The remission of the rest of your sentence here in this place and the destruction of your military crime sheet.'

'Is that all? Go on, Major, you can't expect me to volunteer for some cock-eyed private army and risk my neck for that?' He grinned suddenly. 'I like it here in the glasshouse. After the SOE, it's like a home from home. Besides old Tashy' – he obviously meant the elderly Commandant – 'is like a father to me.'

'What do you want then?' Cain demanded harshly.

'Three things,' Spiv replied. 'Scotch mist up here,' he tapped his sleeve.

'Eh?' Abel queried.

'He means stripes.'

39

'Yeah,' Spiv said. 'Three stripes put you in another class with the Judies, you see Captain. They come across a lot quicker with sergeants than they do with privates. Now if I were an officer and a gent–'

'Get on with it, Spiv.'

'Well, then there's the question of a woman. I've been in here so long now that even the five-fingered widow's getting a bit worn out and I've never gone in much for brown cake. So I need a woman – and fast.'

'You'll get it,' Cain sighed, 'and your last condition?'

'Nothing serious, sir,' the little prisoner said airily, 'I'd just like to say farewell to old Tashy down there.'

'You mean the Commandant?'

'That's right, sir. He's been very good to me, you see and I wouldn't like to go away without offering him my thanks for the way he's attempted to set me straight while I've been in here.'

Cain looked at him suspiciously. But the little Cockney was all innocence, his grey eyes revealing nothing. 'All right then, you're on. I'll see you get promoted. I'll personally conduct you to the most expensive whore in the West End. Now are you satisfied?'

'One hundred per cent,' Spiv answered enthusiastically and stretched out his hand. 'You've got another recruit to Ultra, sir.'

A minute later, towered over by the black-jawed RSM, Spiv stood rigidly to attention in front of the Prison Commandant. While the two Ultra officers and the sweating prisoners stared at him, he rapped loudly, so that everyone could hear, 'Sir, as you know, I am being posted. But before I go I'd like to express my appreciation of the way you've tried to make a good soldier of me again.'

'Well, that's very nice of you to say that, Brooks,' smirked the elderly Commandant and ran his fingers across his moustache, 'very nice indeed.'

'But every word of it's true, sir,' Spiv bellowed, while the spectators listened in wonder. 'You've learned me what wonders drill can work with no-goods like me who have been sent here because of their crimes and misdeeds.'

'Say no more, Brooks, say no more. That was very fulsome praise.'

'But I'd like to say one more thing before I go, sir, if I may?'

'Well, if you must then, Brooks. What is it?'

'Why don't you take that bloody silly little tash off yer silly old face!' Spiv roared, and before anyone could stop him, he wiped the wet handkerchief he had hidden in his clenched fist across the Commandant's mouth, smearing black pencil across the surprised officer's addled old cheeks.

'What the hell are you up to?' bellowed the

RSM above the roar of laughter which swelled up from the rigid ranks of the prisoners. He reached out a big hand and tried to grab the grinning ex-prisoner. Spiv was quicker. He brought up his knee smartly and caught the RSM in the pit of the stomach.

'Christ,' Cain yelled, 'let's get the little bastard out of here before all hell's let loose!'

A moment later the three of them were scattering the ranks of the laughing prisoners to left and right as they ran for the waiting staff car.

FIVE

'They call it Churchill's Toyshop,' said the squat Sapper Major with the humorous face. 'Disparagingly naturally. Because the toys we produce here at the Firs, Major Cain are very dangerous ones. Our tame nihilists see to that, I can assure you.'

'I know, Major,' Cain said. Although he was tired from the long drive from the military prison to the remote, half-timbered house near Aylesbury which housed the hush-hush organisation that had been supplying the SOE with all kinds of cunning explosive devices for the last two years, he was interested to see the place at last.

'This is the Firefly,' the Sapper said, picking up what looked like a plastic cylinder from the display of special weapons in the big entrance hall. 'We supply these to French filling station attendants, working for the Maquis. Put in a Jerry's petrol tank, it explodes miles later when the petrol swells up a rubber retainer ring and no one is the wiser who put the device in. Or what about this, Major Cain? We call this Aunt Jemima. It's a powdered form of TNT.'

'It looks like ordinary wheat flour to me.'

The Sapper laughed. 'That's just what it is intended to look like. If the Gestapo gets suspicious, you can knead it into dough in front of their eyes and bake a cake with it. In fact, you could eat that cake without danger, though it wouldn't be advisable to smoke a cigarette immediately afterwards.'

'What's this?' Cain pointed to what looked like a ring of sausages of the type favoured by continental workmen.

'Bangers,' the Sapper replied with unconcealed pride. 'In both senses of the word. A Maquis could carry that in his hand with a piece of bread, as if he were about to eat it. Then when a Jerry vehicle went by, he could sling it at the thing and run like hell. It's a new kind of sticky grenade. Hence the name – banger.' His face creased with merriment as he put down the diabolical device. 'But I mustn't keep you here, gossiping like this.

43

You want to see Mac at once, I should imagine. He's down at the stables, working as usual. Come on, let me take you to him, Major Cain.'

A couple of minutes later the Sapper Major opened the door to the stables which had been converted into an explosives lab, revealing a tall man with a shock of untidy bright red hair crouched over a table at the far end. 'That's Mac,' he announced in a whisper, 'and his temper is as flaming as his hair. So tread warily, Major Cain.'

'I will. But what's he doing?'

'He's trying to improve the AP Switch.'

'The AP Switch? I've never heard of that one.'

The Sapper chuckled softly. 'I expect you'll know it better as the deballocker. Crude, I know, but it explains its purpose pretty effectively don't you think?'

Cain nodded. He had heard of the device, one of Churchill's Toyshop's most fiendish inventions. Buried in sand or soft soil, it was almost invisible to the naked eye. But when an enemy soldier stood on it, it soon made its presence known. Under the pressure of his foot, a small explosive charged fired the standard 303 bullet right between his outstretched legs with devastating effect. 'Well, Major, perhaps you could leave me alone with Lieutenant MacFarland now.'

'Of course. But remember – watch that

temper of his.'

'I will,' Cain promised as the Sapper slipped out of the lab as silently as he had entered.

For a few moments Cain studied the big red-headed man working at the bench as if he hadn't a moment to spare, noting the powerful bare arms and almost brutal thrust of the shoulder muscles. MacFarland looked a very tough baby indeed, though as he recalled from the Scot's dossier there was nothing in his early record which indicated that he would develop into anything more than a very ordinary if highly skilled mining engineer. But 1940 had changed all that. While he was earning the Military Cross on the beaches of Dunkirk, his wife and two small children were killed by a tip-and-run German raider in Eastbourne.

The death of his family had transformed the Scot into a man who had only one mission in life – to kill Germans. Almost immediately he had volunteered for the SOE and had been sent on several missions in the Middle East where he had distinguished himself by his ruthlessness and mechanical cunning. In 1941 he had been severely wounded when one of his murderous explosive devices had exploded prematurely just as he was about to plant it on a lonely Balkan railway tie. Somehow or other the SOE had managed to get him home and when he had recovered, posted him as an instructor to Station Seventeen. But Mac-Farland had not been able to stick it long at the SOE centre in Herefordshire, where agents were given technical sabotage instruction. He had wanted something more active. Thus, after Gubbins had refused to send him back on ops, he had somehow or other wangled a job at the Firs, experimenting with increasingly deadly destructive devices.

Cain cleared his throat. Nothing happened. Cain waited a moment and then cleared his throat again.

'I hear ye, man,' a thick Scots voice growled. 'Ye don't have to rupture your tonsils. Well, spit it out. Say yer piece and be on yer way. I've no time to waste.'

'I prefer to see the face of the man I'm talking to, Lieutenant MacFarland, if you don't mind.'

'Och man,' MacFarland said, 'I dinna have time for yon peacetime niceties. Can ye no see I've got a problem on my hands? I'm trying to work out the correct angle to set the bullet so that whatever way the bluidy German stands on it, it'll rip his balls off every single time!' There was a barely restrained savagery about the way he said the last words and Cain told himself that he wouldn't like to be any German, who fell into the Scot's hamlike hands.

'Lieutenant MacFarland, I think I can

offer you a job which will rip the balls off more Germans than a whole trainload of those deballockers of yours.'

MacFarland stiffened. The deadly little metal device dropped from his hands on to the bench with a slight clatter. He began to turn slowly and Cain could see why Gubbins had not sent MacFarland on ops again for nearly a year now. His whole red face was peppered by a mass of black dots, with the one eye blurred and twisted at an odd angle. Incongruously enough, a monocle was screwed in the other, which glared a bright angry blue eye, sizing Cain up.

'Ay, ay, I know well, man. You don't have to say it,' MacFarland growled. 'I'm no bluidy oil painting and this glass window in my eye makes me look like one of yon chinless wonders P.G. Wodehouse used to write about before the war. But without it, I'm as blind as a bat.' Without giving Cain time to recover MacFarland snapped. 'Now then what did you just say about my being given a chance to kill more Germans than a trainload of those little beauties behind me could?'

Cain pulled himself together swiftly, and grinned. The man was certainly no respecter of persons or rank, but he was very definitely single-minded in his desire to kill the enemy. Quickly he explained the details of his new unit, while the other man nodded his head from time to time. When Cain had finished, he thrust his mutilated, angry face close to Cain's.

'I've got just one question to ask you man,' he growled, 'before I give ye my answer. When is yon Ultra gonna start killing Germans?'

'We start on operations tomorrow, Mac-Farland.'

The Scot thrust out a hamlike fist covered by long red hairs. 'Then I'm yer man, Major.'

SIX

The green light blinked. 'All right, Cain, in you go,' Zero C said. 'The big Chief is waiting for you – and he doesn't like to be kept waiting.'

Together the two of them went into the big office in the Queen Anne's Gate HQ of the SIS and for the first time, Cain saw the man who headed the Service, the mysterious 'C' about whom he had heard so many rumours these last few years.

'The Major, I told you about,' Zero C said, 'Cain, the man we picked to head the new Ultra unit.'

C was a pale thin man in his mid-fifties with light blond hair and faded blue eyes, the only splash of colour in his whole appearance his Old Etonian tie. For what seemed a long time he did not speak, silently sizing Cain up. Finally he said, 'All right, you may go, Zero C.'

C waited until the padded, leather-covered door had closed behind the other man, then he pressed the button which activated the red light outside and indicated that he was engaged.

'Major Cain,' he said, without slightest ceremony. 'In two months' time the Western Allies will finally go over to the offensive in Europe. A dual Anglo-American task force, sailing from the UK and the United States will initiate Operation Torch, the capture of the French territories in North Africa. Once they are established there, Rommel and his *Afrika Korps* will be faced with a battle on two fronts. Thereupon we will be ready to launch an attack on Europe proper. On Italy. Clear?'

'Clear sir.'

'Now it is very obvious from the Ultra intercepts that the Hun has cottoned on to the fact that we're up to something. We've already picked up Enigma signals indicating that he is moving fresh troops down to Italy, Sardinia and Greece. It is clear that the Hun thinks we're going to have a crack at him somewhere or other in the Med. Only, for-tunately enough, he's got the wrong coast. So far, therefore, we seem safe in North Africa because naturally the French territories there are still being run by Vichy.' He looked out the big French window at the barrage balloons tethered in the park beyond.

Cain frowned. He could understand already why Zero C did not like this pale reticent man who obviously treated his employees as if they were pieces on a chessboard to be moved about at will.

Finally C took his faded blue eyes off the balloons. 'A month ago we picked up a message addressed to all commands from Field Marshal Keitel asking for them to put forward names of fit men who spoke Spanish. The men in question were to report for special duties at the *Adolf Hitler Kaserne* at the small Eifel town of Wittlich not far from the French border.' C sighed. 'A week later the Bletchley boffins noted the transfer of *General der Luftwaffe* Hans Meyer from the Führer's Reserve of General Officers to Trier, some twenty miles away from Wittlich. Do you see anything significant in that now, Major?'

Cain shook his head firmly; he was not going to let himself be intimidated by this strange pale man. 'No sir, except the fact that it is strange to transfer an Air Force general to a town which does not have a military air field within twenty-five miles of it as far as I can recall.'

'Good, good,' C said, fiddling with his pen

again. (Later Cain was to learn that this was always a sign in C of inner excitement.) 'We thought the same – and more. You see *General der Luftwaffe* Meyer once enjoyed another name – *el Lobo Gris*. Though at his present weight of some three hundred pounds, one could hardly call him the "grey wolf" today.'

'You mean that Meyer once had something to do with Spain and that is the connection with the Spanish speaking volunteers at the other place,' Cain clicked his fingers impatiently. 'Wittlich?'

'That's right. In 1937, during the Civil War in Spain, he was the deputy commander of the German volunteers on Franco's side, the Condor Legion. Then he was shot down by Communist guerrillas in Catalonia, and it took Franco and the Huns twenty thousand pounds in gold to buy him back after a month in their hands.'

'I see, sir. But what has all this got to do with Torch?'

'Well, our people have discovered that El Lobo Gris has a passionate hatred of all things Spanish, due probably to his experience in the Communists' hands. For example we heard that he was offered a senior post with the Blue Legion while they found their feet in Russia last winter. But he turned it down, telling that feller Hitler to his face that he would sooner resign his

51

commission than have anything to do with the Spanish. So what does one make of the posting of an Air Force general, who hates Spaniards with a passion, to an area where there are no military airfields but a large number of Spanish-speaking volunteers?

'We were as puzzled as you probably are, Major until two weeks ago, when Ultra picked up a signal directed to the head of the *Abwehr* in Spain, a man called Lentz. Here, have a look at it yourself.' He pushed over a flimsy piece of paper with the word ULTRA printed in bold red letters across the top.

'Detail main entry routes to Seville where terrain might cause difficulties: the western route from Bordeaux through Irun to Almendralejo; the eastern route via Perpignan through Sitges to Valencia. *Most immediate* – all possible details of Seville Air Field and alternative sites if Field destroyed. Canaris.'

C gave him a moment to absorb the information, then he said, 'As the message came from Admiral Canaris, the head of the *Abwehr,* we realised that it was a top priority and it–'

'Started you off wondering why the Germans were so interested in Seville?'

'Right. We soon found the answer. With Seville in their hands, the Huns could soon render Gibraltar virtually untenable as a naval base, with the Air Force at their disposal – they've obviously spotted our build up for Torch there. The railway line between Casablanca, the Americans' main supply port for Torch, and Algiers would be well within range of their Seville based planes.'

'You mean that the Germans are contemplating occupation of Spain?'

'All things seem to point to that. The Meyer organisation being built up on the Franco-German border at Trier, the *Abwehr's* interest into the two main entry routes into Spain and in Seville.'

'But Franco is Germany's ally,' Cain objected.

'To an extent,' C mused, fiddling with his pen again. 'But so far, Hitler had not been able to convince him to join in the war on the side of the Axis. And we have no clear indication of what his reaction would be if the Germans attempted to occupy his country or even ask for military facilities once the Torch landings had taken place. But whether he resisted or not the Germans would win in the end, and with Seville in their hands, they could make it damnably difficult for our people in North Africa.' His voice rose and he stared hard at Cain. 'Therefore we cannot allow the Hun to occupy that part of Spain. We must be prepared to carry out the first Ultra operation – to nip the whole business in the bud.'

'How sir?' Cain asked, knowing as he posed the question what the other man's answer would be.

'By killing the Grey Wolf.'

He pressed the button on his desk. Outside the green light began to burn again. The interview was over.

SEVEN

'All right you Joes,' ordered the RAF type with the fruity voice, as the truck which had brought them from London drew away from the guardroom at RAF Tempsford, 'follow me please.'

Obediently the Ultra team, already clad in their nondescript civilian clothes, trooped after him under the suspicious gaze of the sentries. 'Good old 138 Squadron,' Spiv said, shaking his head. 'Same old drill, back to being Joes again.'

'Kinda funny to have an airfield used for clandestine ops smack bang close to the main railroad from Norwich to London,' Abel remarked and indicated the darkened express rushing south.

'That's exactly why we chose it,' the RAF type said, 'we reckoned that no one in his right mind would suspect us of carrying out secret ops from a place so open as this – too obvious.'

'Go on,' Spiv said sourly. 'Tell that one to the Marines. They might believe it.'

'Close that dirty mouth of yours,' Mac growled, doubling his big fist, 'or I'll belt ye one.'

The RAF type sniffed.

'All right,' he opened the door to the hangar. 'In we go for a little bit of slap and tickle.'

Four hard-eyed RAF corporals were already waiting for them, their faces stony.

'Rozzers,' Spiv said to Abel in no way abashed by Mac's threat. 'I can smell 'em a mile off.'

The tallest of the four opened a mouth which seemed to be worked by a steel spring, 'Would you mind raising your arms please gentlemen. We would like to do the search now.'

'Search us?' queried Abel, the only one of the four who had not been through the standard procedure before.

'Yes, to check we haven't overlooked anything that might incriminate us on the other side,' Cain explained, raising his arms obediently.

Swiftly and expertly the four ex-policemen carried out the search and found nothing. 'Wizard show,' the RAF type said. 'All right, follow me you Joes for stage two.'

Outside it was growing dark now, and airmen were already beginning to put up the blackout blinds in the huts. Somewhere a gramophone was playing an old scratchy recording of the Cab Calloway band blasting out the *One O'Clock Jump.*

Spiv sighed as they trooped towards the next hangar. 'They'll already be jiving at the Norwich Palais. All that lovely grub, having to do without me.' He nudged an amused Abel. 'You know what Norwich means, don't you, Yank?'

'No.'

'Knickers off, ready and waiting!'

Ahead of them the RAF type said. 'Don't worry about that, Joe. When you lot are off on your little ride, I'll zoom down there and take care of the knickers-off types. Wizzo!'

'Ballocks!' was Spiv's reply.

Inside the great echoing hangar the four of them found their flying gear already neatly laid out for them on a long trestle table. 'Striptease suits, rubber helmets, spine pads, everything the heart desires,' the RAF type announced cheerfully, 'and a nice assortment of deadly weapons.'

'Ay man, now yer talking,' Mac said eagerly, picking up a 45 Colt and a trench knife, its grip fashioned to make a handy if ugly knuckleduster. He thrust his hand through the metal holes and growled. 'With this thing you could give some Jerry a bad case of toothache, I'll be bound.'

With difficulty they began to draw on the

aptly named striptease suits and stow their weapons and escape compasses. Parachutes and rubber helmets followed. Finally the RAF type was satisfied. 'One last thing, Joes. A couple of little presents, compliments of the 138th Squadron.' He opened the briefcase he had been carrying with him all the time and brought out four small metal flasks and handed them each one. 'To be used at the other end, please – customs regulations you know.'

'What is it?' Abel asked curiously, accepting his.

'Whisky,' Cain explained, sweating heavily in the cumbersome gear which enclosed him like a suit of armour. 'They always give you whisky as a parting gift.'

'And one other thing, Joes,' the RAF type said, reaching in his attaché case once more. 'Your L-pills. Cyanide, old boy. Just in case you get into a tricky situation and there's no other way out. L for lethal, you see.'

Thirty minutes later the pilot opened the throttle of the four-engined Halifax. Slowly the converted bomber started to roll forward. The roar of the engines grew louder. The plane began to vibrate. The air grew colder. Suddenly that old familiar light, thin feeling beneath his feet told Cain that they were airborne. They were on their way.

He glanced around his men sprawled out

in the tight belly of the plane, filled with packages, protected with thick wads of sponge rubber and with the parachutes already attached to them. Their pale faces showed no emotion. He nodded his satisfaction at their lack of apprehension and sinking back into his canvas chair he closed his eyes with a sigh of relief.

While the Halifax ploughed its way steadily eastwards over a blacked-out England, already settling down to the Home Service on the radio and Tommy Handley's ITMA show, he reviewed the events of the last few hectic days since C had given him Ultra's first assignment. The reaction of his three recruits to the news of their mission had been different yet in character. Abel, the good guy, had looked at him sharply and snapped: 'You mean murder this general – *in cold blood?*' To which Mac had growled, as if that were explanation enough. 'But yon man's a bluidy Jerry, isn't he, Yank!' Spiv's reaction had been: 'What's in it for us, Major?'

Cain had answered, half amused, half repelled by the little Cockney's avarice. 'We'll see you get some promotion out of it. Would the rank of field marshal suit you perhaps?'

But after the initial surprise at hearing what their assignment was to be, and the fact that they would be the first British agents to take clandestine warfare into Germany itself, they had soon settled down to their preparations.

As Ultra had no information to the location of the Grey Wolf's HQ in Trier, Abel, the ex-professor, had scoured London's libraries until he had found *Meyer's Konversation-slexion.*

'Under each city heading,' he explained, 'it gives a condensed description of the place's important public buildings, the sort of thing you won't find in Baedeker or the usual tourist guidebooks.'

While the others had crowded around him curiously, he had leafed through the dusty pages. 'Here we are – Trier. Let's see what they say. Hm, the Bishop's Palace? No, hardly. The barracks of the Fourth Trier Infantry Regiment,' he looked up curiously at Cain.

'No, Abel. The Grey Wolf will probably only have a small staff, so what would he need a barracks for. Besides if he is engaged in a clandestine op, he wouldn't want a barracks in the centre of town. Look for something a little more remote if you can.'

'What about this then?' Abel had asked a moment later. *'PH Trier?* Trier's *Padagogische Hochschule* – the local teacher training college for girls. The place is located just outside Trier on the Moselle on a high and … er … little inaccessible cliff. Look there's a picture of the place.' He had held up the book for them all to see.

'That could be it,' Cain had said thoughtfully, staring at the poor illustration of a plain white building sited at the edge of a sandstone cliff which rose steeply from the Moselle below. 'It's the sort of place one would pick for a clandestine headquarters.'

'Looks like a damned fortress to me,' Mac had growled. 'But dinna worry, I could blast my way into it without too much difficulty. A wee parcel of plastic explosive here–'

'Why blast,' Spiv had interrupted. 'With my charm and the way I've got with the Judies, I could walk in through the front gate, mate.'

In the end, Cain had decided that unless they learned anything to the contrary, they would regard the teacher training college on the cliff as the most likely site for the Grey Wolf's HQ. That settled, he had started to tackle the problem of where he would direct 138 Squadron to land Ultra to start off their operation. Germany, he had decided straight away, was completely out of the question, although Trier was located not too far from the remote Eifel region, where houses and villages were few and far between. But he didn't want to take the chance of dropping blind into enemy country, where the slightest mistake could and would alert the entire security service. They must parachute into Allied territory, Belgium or France, yet close enough for it not to become too much of a problem to get to Trier with the equipment they would have to take with them.

It was then that he had begun to run into problems. Neither the Belgian nor the French SOE sections could help him. Both of the sections had no organisations in the French Lorraine area, close to the German border, or in the Belgian East Cantons, which made up the frontier with the Reich further north.

'You see,' he had explained to his men. 'The Lorraine was once German territory and there are too many Frenchmen in the area stretching from Metz to the German frontier who feel they owe an allegiance to the Nazis. That, apparently, has made it too dangerous for the French Section to start up a Maquis organisation in the area – that and the fact that it is a highly industrialised area with few hideouts suitable for the Maquis. Now further north here,' he had pointed to Eastern Belgium on the map, 'the terrain is much more suitable for clandestine ops. It's a rugged, lonely wooded area – the Ardennes. Unfortunately for us, it belonged to Germany until we took it off them after the First World War and the population is totally German-speaking. Indeed in 1940 when the Nazis conquered Belgium, Hitler decreed that the people of the Eastern Cantons, as they are called, are *Reichsdeutsche* and as far as I can gather, many thousands of them are already serving in the German Army. Understandably *l'Armee Blanche,* the Belgian Maquis, have had little success in getting anything started east of the River Meuse – here. No,' he had concluded glumly, 'I'm afraid the Belgian Ardennes are out of the question as a DZ.'

One day later Major Cain had been proved wrong. Late that afternoon, a bespectacled Captain in the Intelligence Corps had been ushered into his office and introduced himself as 'Captain Smithers of X Section, SOE.'

'X Section – never heard of it.'

'No, neither has anyone else, Major,' the young officer had confided.

'You see I'm the total staff on this side of the water.'

'But what country are you working?' Cain had asked somewhat mystified.

'Germany.'

'What!' Cain had exploded.

'Yes, though so far we're not doing so well. Understandably the Germans are not standing in line exactly to join the SOE.'

Cain had laughed.

'But we have managed to recruit a small number of *Reichsdeutsche* from the Eupen area who are definitely anti-Nazi – and they're prepared to provide you with a DZ.'

'Where?'

The Captain had pointed to the map of Eastern Belgium on Cain's desk. 'Here at Baraque Michel. It's the highest point of the Ardennes – over two thousand feet – and easy for recognition purposes. It's lonely too. There are no houses within a radius of a couple of miles.'

'Sounds just the job,' Cain had said enthusiastically.

'There's a catch though, Major,' the other man had hesitated. 'Because the place is so high and open it is plagued by high winds, which if your pilot doesn't drop you exactly on the DZ, could carry you into the marshy area – here. With your equipment and the difficulty of freeing yourself from the chute, well you know what I mean.'

'Yes, I know.' For a few moments Cain had considered, then he had made his decision. 'Captain, I'll take you up on your offer. You're on.' He had forced a grin. 'But those boys of the 138th had better be right on the target, eh?'

Now they were on the way and as the Halifax swept across the coast and headed for the Continent, Cain started to drift into an uneasy sleep in which he fought against muddy hands that attempted to drag him down into a nameless, black-bubbling morass.

Cain awoke to a sound resembling a gigantic bird tapping its beak against the thin metal shell of the Halifax. It was the noise of exploding shells.

'Flak,' Spiv said calmly. 'Here we go again. Old Jerry wants us to feel welcome.'

'Ruddy awful shots,' Mac grunted unperturbed. 'Couldn't hit a bluidy barn door–'

Suddenly the Halifax's engines cut out. The plane side-slipped wildly and they clutched for a hold. For one frightening second, Cain thought they would have to bale out there and then. Then the engines roared into life again and the pilot brought the Halifax back on course. Spiv breathed a long sigh of heartfelt relief.

'What did you say about not being able to hit a barn door, Mac?'

Ten minutes later they had left the coastal flak and searchlights behind them, and were rapidly approaching the dropping zone. The sergeant dispatcher came awkwardly down the plane. Bending down, he opened the hatch, flooding the Halifax with cold air. Looking at the men of Ultra, he held up one hand, fingers outstretched. Cain nodded. Five minutes to the DZ.

'All right,' he cried above the noise, 'hook up your static lines. I'm going first.'

Clambering over the packages which would be dropped to the German Maquis after them, he hooked up his static line and positioned himself with his back to the engines, legs dangling out of the hole. Abel squatted next to him; he would jump as number two. Together they waited in silence. Slowly the Halifax began to lose speed. Cain craned his neck. He could see nothing below, just darkness. Presumably up ahead, the pilot had seen the lights outlining the DZ. Yes, suddenly the red light flashed on.

The sergeant dispatcher raised his arm, his eyes fixed on the light. Cain tensed. He tried to give Abel a smile of encouragement. Abel's face was pale but resolute. Cain knew what must be going on inside his head; this was his first combat jump.

'Don't forget the diver,' Spiv broke the tension with the famous lines from ITMA. 'Going down now, sir.'

Cain grinned and at that moment the light changed to green. The sergeant dispatcher's hand came down on his shoulder. Automatically he heaved himself forward. The wind slapped him in the face. Thrown round, his head struck the Halifax's tail wind. He grunted with pain. Stars exploded before his eyes. Cain blacked out.

When he came round, he was swinging from side to side, his shroudlines a tangled mess, the Halifax a hard, black silhouette outlined against the silver sky. But Cain had no time to check if the others had already jumped. As the Intelligence Corps Captain had predicted, a strong wind was blowing hard and bearing him away from the ring of lights which was the DZ.

He tugged at the shroudlines with his hook. A small farm loomed up on his right. He pulled at the lines again. He didn't want to land near there. Farms always had dogs and once they started barking, they'd alert half of Belgium. The farm faded away. A violent gust of wind caught him and he felt himself being driven across the height at full speed. Instinctively he tensed, drawing up his knees to protect himself better, as a wood rushed up to meet him.

The wind carried him right into it. Twigs slapped at his face. His nostrils filled with the heavy scent of pine as he crashed through the trees. A branch snapped back and hit him in the face. Again he blacked out momentarily. When he came to, he was leaving the pines behind him and dropping rapidly towards a bare stretch of open heathland.

With a sudden feeling of horror, he realised that he was heading for the swampland that the Captain had warned him about. Desperately he fought with the shroudlines, tugging frantically, trying to empty the chute of air so that he would drop before he hit the marsh, but the wind carried him relentlessly towards it. Somewhere he had read that the only way to save oneself in a swamp was to lie flat on one's face and progress forward as if swimming. As soon as he came down, therefore, he must release the chute and roll on to his belly. His plan made, he played out the air with one hand and clutched the other to the release catch, ready to ditch the chute as soon as he touched the swamp.

Twenty feet, ten. He could already smell the heavy odour of stale swamp water. Five feet. He took a deep breath. This was it. As his boots hit the water, he hit the quick-release catch. As the chute collapsed all around him, he twisted round and flung himself forward into the stinking morass and lay absolutely still, arms spread in front of him, as if he were about to start swimming, fighting his inclination to panic. For what seemed an eternity, he lay there feeling the water beginning to penetrate his jump suit and hearing the soft squelch of the mud as his body started to settle into it. Then with a supreme effort of will, he forced himself to move. Slowly, he moved his right arm and gripped the edge of the white canopy which lay across his back. The mud quaked alarmingly. He stopped instantly. He steeled himself. Gingerly he started to draw the chute over his head. All around him the mud groaned and sighed as if it were a live thing.

Finally he had done it. The chute lay spread out in front of him covering a couple of square yards or so of the swamp. With a grunt Cain raised his head and surveyed the immediate area. Some five or six feet beyond the chute there was a clump of coarse grass. That could indicate solid ground, he told himself. But at that particular moment, it seemed as far away from him as did the stars gleaming high above in the night sky. Cain drew a deep breath. It was now or never.

He began to squirm on to the chute. The stinking mire sucked greedily at his body. Grimly he fought the mud. It stuck to him like glue, making every movement a mortal fight.

Now he had the whole of his upper body on the chute, which, although it was sagging alarmingly in the middle, was still keeping the mud and water out. Inch after inch, he slithered forward, the mud fighting him tenaciously, dragging at his legs as he propelled himself through the swamp. And then he had made it and was lying on the silk, his chest heaving wildly.

Far away he could make out faint shouts like men calling to each other over distances. Perhaps it was the reception party looking for him, he thought. But it might well be someone else and he knew he daren't risk shouting for help. He would have to fight his way to the clump of grass alone.

He raised his head carefully and eyed the grass. It looked firm, and in contrast to the bright green of the obviously marshy grass near it, it was yellow and coarse, as if it were growing on dry soil. He said a silent prayer that his guess was right and started his slow progress across the chute. It bubbled and squelched alarmingly beneath him and the water began to seep in on both sides, but still it held. At the far end, he paused and took another deep breath.

Cain was just over six foot and the tuft of yellow grass was about eight foot away. He did a quick calculation as the shouts came closer. If he dived forward, arms spread out, with his fingers extended to their full length, he might be just able to grasp the yellow tuft. But if he missed or lost his initial hold, the impact of his dive would surely force him beneath the stinking black mud which oozed and bubbled so horrifyingly in front of him. What was he going to do? Should he take the chance?

'*Hierdrueben… Ich glaube der Mann ist hierdrueben gelandet,*' the voice shouted not more than a hundred yards away, carrying far on the still night air.

The shout made Cain's mind up for him. He couldn't understand the words at that distance, but he could recognise the language all right. It was German. He had to make the attempt to get away while there was still time.

Cain sucked in air and closed his mouth firmly. Mentally he counted to three. With a deep grunt he sprang forward like a champion diver launching himself from the edge of a pool. He hit the mud with his full weight. It splattered up on both sides and he sank in up to his ribs. The stink of the mud filled his nostrils as it welled up below his chin and he grabbed for the tuft. Blinded, but frantic with fear, he found it and caught hold. *Would it give?* the terrifying thought shot through his mind.

But the tuft held, its roots dug deeply into the dry earth below it. Cain could have cried out with relief at that moment. But the shouts were getting closer and the mud would have filled his mouth had he done so. Instead, summoning up the last of his strength, he dug his hook into the earth as an anchor and with his good hand, started to haul himself out of the tenaciously clinging mire sucking greedily at his legs.

His shoes went, dragged off his feet by the suction. The mud tore at his flying suit. He fought back, the sweat pouring down his red face, his eyes bulging from their sockets. The strain on his shoulder muscles was unbearable. He dug his teeth into his bottom lip in order to prevent himself from crying out. He could hear someone wading cautiously through water now, not fifty yards away.

With the blood from his bottom lip streaming down his bemired chin, he made one last effort. The mud belched obscenely; suddenly the suction vanished and he was free, sprawled on the little island of firm ground, sobbing with relief, his body trembling uncontrollably, not even able to call out in his exhaustion to the deep woman's voice, which kept repeating the same old cry *'C'est vous, Ultra? ... c'est vous Ultra?...'*

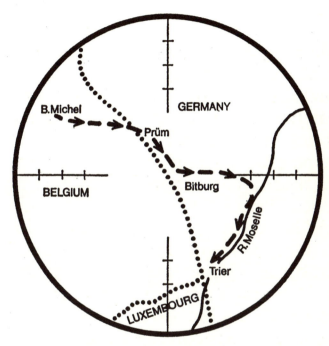

A PASSAGE TO TRIER (August 1942)

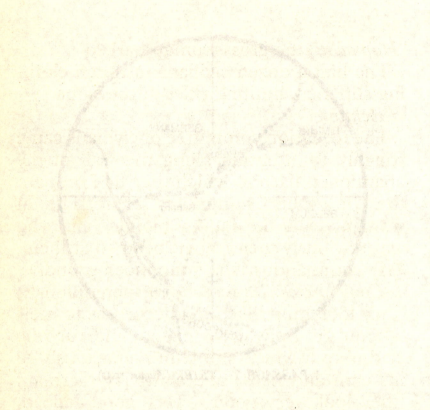

ONE

'*Hab acht!*' the gross woman barked.

The half a dozen civilians in rough clothing stiffened, hunting rifles at the slope.

'*Achtung!*'

The reception committee of civilians came roughly to attention along the wall of the abandoned barn to which they had brought the Ultra men five minutes before. The fat woman, with the fading blonde hair who was obviously their leader, beamed at them. 'My commandos,' she announced proudly.

'*Commandos,*' Spiv echoed incredulously, 'they look more like bloody corpses to me!'

'Shut up, Spiv,' Cain hissed, and rubbing at the mud which still clung tenaciously to his chin and neck, said slowly in German, 'they look very good – very good indeed, Frau, er...'

'Call me Rosi – *Fat* Rosi,' the woman answered and chuckled so that her tremendous breasts trembled like puddings underneath her loose blouse. 'Everyone else does on account of this.' She drew her two hands the length of her massive body which must have weighed all of two hundred pounds.

Cain nodded. 'All right, er ... Rosi, please

73

stand your commandos at–'

'Ease,' Abel supplied the word in his more fluent German.

'Ruhrt euch!' she barked and the civilians with the rough, red faces of farmworkers relaxed. 'Now,' she continued, 'there is food.' She pointed to the pile of black bread sandwiches heaped on the trestle table next to the hissing petroleum lamp. 'With best Ardennes ham – cost a fortune on the black market in Eupen.'

Mac was first to react. 'Ay, I could do with a bite. That night air makes a man hungry. And what about a dram?' He brought out the flask and offered the 138th's whisky to the strangely shy men lining the wall of the barn which smelled of animal droppings, boiled cabbage and human sweat. 'Whisky,' he said loudly, as if the louder he spoke, the quicker the German Maquisards would understand.

Hesitantly the nearest man picked it up and took a sip. He coughed and spluttered at the fiery liquid and the others laughed; their shyness was broken and the Ultra men, aided by the woman started on the food.

For a while they ate in silence while Cain observed the woman, who concentrated single-mindedly on the food, rubbing her left breast all the time, as if she were kneading dough. With her faded blonde hair, flat round face and heavy figure she seemed to him to be as German as *Sauerkraut und Eisbein*. Why should she risk her life helping them when her fellow-countrymen dominated the whole of Europe from the Urals to the Channel?

The huge woman answered his question indirectly a little later. Taking a swig from Mac's flask, her mouth still full of black bread and ham, she said ponderously, 'We have been asked by London to help you. As you can see,' she took her plump, dimpled hand from her breast and indicated the others lounging in the flickering shadows cast by the petroleum lamp, 'we are not many and we are just at the beginning. But we will do our best, I promise you.'

Cain had already decided that he would tell her so much, but not the complete truth. Even if she were genuine, as he thought she was, she would be forced to sing if she ever fell into the Gestapo's hands – and he could not risk that. 'Thank you. I know you will. You see, we want to get across the border into the Reich as soon as possible.'

Fat Rosi looked at him startled, her open mouth full of food. 'There are many who want to *leave* the Reich, refugees from the war factories, deserters, our own POWs who have escaped from German camps. But I've never heard of anyone attempting *to get into* the country.' She shrugged and her massive breasts trembled. 'But it can be done; there is no border now between the East Cantons and Germany. All of us here are German again.

'We were born German, then in nineteen you made us Belgians, now the Führer has made us German again. If only they would leave us alone to go our own ways in peace – the lot of them, Belgians and Germans!'

'Is that why you are risking your lives to help us?' Abel asked.

Fat Rosi nodded and picked up another sandwich absently. 'I suppose,' she answered. 'I was born German and now I am German again. But what good has it done me – or the rest of us here in the East Cantons either? They took my father and killed him on the Somme in sixteen. Last year they took my husband and murdered him before Moscow. In the end they'll take all our menfolk, perhaps even the women too, and slaughter us all. Cannon fodder, that is what we have been for those in Berlin in two wars.' Her fat face flushed angrily. 'And what do you think we get for it afterwards?'

Abel shook his head.

'After the first war, the Belgians, our new masters, treated us as third-class citizens. We weren't even represented in the Senate in Brussels. But when Germany loses this second war – and she will, with half the world fighting against her – we in the East Cantons don't want to be third-class citizens again. But we must do something about it. We must fight for our own rights – that's why we're helping you.'

There was a mumble of agreement from the others.

Fat Rosi pushed the platter of sandwiches to one side and spread a faded large-scale map of the border area over the table. 'We are here,' she stabbed the map with her forefinger. 'Prior to 1940 the border with the Reich used to run here.'

Spiv standing next to her nodded. 'Yes, I remember it well. I've come across from Prum there to St Vith many a time.'

She looked down at him curiously. 'Are you a Jew?' she asked.

He clapped his hand to his big nose. 'Na, don't think that makes me one of the few, Rosi. All my organs happen to be big,' he winked at her, 'that's all.'

'Let's get on with it,' Cain interrupted irritably.

The fat woman took her eyes, suddenly full of interest, from the little Cockney's face and looked down at the map again. 'We will start early, just before dusk tomorrow evening. We will arrange a truck to take you as far as Bullingen – here. From there we shall start cross-country, making our way through the woods towards the frontier and pass it – here – between Manderfeld and Schonberg. As I said, there is no official border any more, but the police sometimes run occasional patrols in the area after dark to look for escaped POWs and deserters trying to make their way back to the East Cantons and the like. But mostly the police around here are old and fat – they'll stick to the roads.'

'And who will be the guide?' Spiv asked. 'Those frontier forests are pretty dense.'

The woman looked down at him and poked a finger like a sausage at her left bosom. 'Fat Rosi of course – who else?' She beamed at him. 'But now you must sleep, while we stand guard. That is, if you all want to sleep?' She looked pointedly at the little Cockney.

Spiv paled. 'Jesus Christ,' he breathed to Abel in English. 'She likes me, all that meat and no potatoes. Heaven help a sailor on a night like this!'

Abel grinned. 'It pays to be good,' he quipped.

'Yes, but not too much,' Cain snapped, pointing to the bundles of old straw at the far end of the abandoned barn. 'All right, come on the lot of you, get your heads down. You're not going to get much sleep in the days to come.' He nudged Spiv with his hook. 'And I mean everybody, Spiv. So don't get any fancy ideas.'

Spiv grinned and reluctantly took his cheeky eyes off Rosi's huge breasts. 'God, sir, but I'd need a ladder to get at that one there.'

But despite his exhaustion, Cain could not sleep. He kept reliving those terrible minutes with the sound of the voices speaking the enemy tongue getting ever closer, while he fought his lone battle in the darkness with the mud. Besides him in the hay, Mac and Spiv snored happily, veterans as they were – yesterday forgotten, tomorrow still to come. But from the rustle of the dry summer grass to his right, he could tell that Abel could not sleep either. Nerves, he concluded. After all, the young American was on his first mission and however much combat he had experienced in Spain, that was long ago and could not be compared with the risks of clandestine warfare where every man's hand was against you and the slightest slip did not result simply in the POW camp, but in the firing squad.

'Why didn't you tell her everything – Fat Rosi, I mean?' Abel's disembodied voice floated through darkness, as if he had sensed that Cain was not asleep either.

'Why should I?'

'Because she's a simple honest country-woman risking her life for us – and those other guys too,' Abel answered.

'She only needs to know that we intend to cross the border into Germany. Anything else might prove too dangerous for us. The less she knows, the better.'

Cain could sense Abel's anger. 'But then we're treating her like the Krauts do, Cain,' he hissed. 'Like cannon fodder. Let her make her own decision whether she wants to take the risk of knowing more or not.'

Cain was silent. Outside the only sound was that of a night bird in the forest and the soft cough of one of Rosi's commandos on sentry duty. Finally the one-armed Major spoke. 'Abel,' he said softly. 'Abel, I've been fighting this kind of war since Palestine in thirty-six. It's not been a nice war, but it has taught me one thing.'

'And?'

'Don't trust anybody. You can't afford to in this kind of business – it's too risky.'

Abel caught his breath. 'But what's the value of it all? What are we fighting for – if we can't trust the masses, put them in the big picture. Hell, Cain,' he hissed, 'that isn't democracy.'

Cain laughed softly. 'Do you think that is what we are fighting for – democracy?'

'Sure, of course, I do,' Abel retorted hotly. On Cain's other side, Mac snorted in his sleep and turned noisily. Abel lowered his voice. 'That's why I went to Spain in thirty-seven and that's why I joined the OSS. Because I think we're fighting for a better kind of world than the Nazis can offer the ordinary Joe in the street.'

Cain shook his head in the darkness. 'No,

Abel, we're fighting this war for power and control. Whether the Nazis or whether we, the British and Americans, and probably your Russian friends too, rule the roost after it's all over. That's what we're fighting for. As for your masses, they're sheep. What have the masses in France, Holland, Belgium here, England or America, done to stop Hitler since 1939? Bugger all!' He forced himself to lower his voice. 'It's the few – people like ourselves, the specialists, the experts, the ones prepared to go it alone – who will win this war. And it will be the same people who will run things after it is over. It's always been that way in the past and personally I can't see any reason why it should be any different in the future. In short, we and people like us, are the ones who are important. The rest must be prepared to make sacrifices for us, be cannon fodder, as the woman said, if necessary.'

'Jesus, Cain,' Abel breathed, as if he could not believe his own ears, 'what a goddam cynic you are!'

'Maybe,' Cain grunted and rolled over on his side, 'but I'm still a live one.'

TWO

It was dusk when they moved out into the forest east of the little frontier village of Bullingen, soon leaving the straggle of white-painted, half-timbered cottages behind them, windows already tightly shuttered, ready for the blackout.

Despite her bulk and her age, Fat Rosi set a hot pace, chewing sandwich after sandwich as she strode down the forest trail, her appetite apparently insatiable.

As Spiv cracked behind her back, 'Where the hell does she put all that nosh? She must have bloody hollow legs!'

But while the others laughed at the little Cockney's sally, Cain's dark face remained serious and worried. To him there seemed something eerie, almost uncanny about the green gloom of the fir forest. He was reminded of the old days with Wingate in Palestine, when his senses had been sharper, more acute and he had been able to detect Arab raiders or Jewish arms smugglers from miles away. Although Fat Rosi had assured him the old border was unguarded, he felt instinctively now that there was someone – whether friend or foe, he didn't know –

waiting for them ahead.

The air began to grow colder as they climbed higher through the wooded hills which marched towards the German frontier like a battalion of spiked-helmeted, old-time soldiers. Now everything was dark, lit only by the cold silver cast by the stars above. Finally the woman called a short halt.

As they settled down on the pine needles at the side of the trail gratefully, she took a bite at yet another black bread sandwich and said, 'We're five kilometres from the old frontier now. As far as we know, the only place where we might bump into a patrol is on the road I told you about.'

'Well Rosi,' Spiv said. 'I hope you're right. But in the old days, we learned always to be careful of the Germans. It happened more than once that we thought we were safely in Belgium, to find the Germans had sneaked a patrol across into Belgian territory and–' he hesitated and turned to Abel. 'How do you say in German, Yank, "we had to pick up our knickers and run for it"?'

But the woman had apparently understood. 'Don't worry,' she said confidently, her mouth full of bread and sausage, 'all the young men have gone into the army. The old ones who are left just want a quiet life. They won't cause any trouble. They might patrol the road, perhaps even the heights where they can get to them through the firebreaks.

But not the forest – that's too strenuous for the poor old boys.'

But despite the ease with which the others accepted their situation, Cain remained unconvinced, plagued by his sixth sense. Neither the woman's confidence nor Mac's assurance that he could deal with any elderly German policeman they might bump into, could dispel this deep-rooted feeling of apprehension.

Five minutes later they set off again on the last leg of the journey, with the woman in the lead, followed by Mac, his Colt already drawn, and Cain bringing up the rear, lagging some five yards behind the rest, as prescribed by the usual drill.

Now the night-time silence had taken on a new character. Or so it seemed to Cain. It had an odd brooding quality about it which gave him the eerie sensation that they were being followed. Twice Cain battled with the desire to look behind him and lost. But when he threw an anxious look over his shoulder, there was nothing there but the waving silver shadows. 'Silly bugger,' he cursed under his breath. 'Now stop it, for God's sake, will you!'

They crossed the narrow winding frontier road without difficulty. It was empty. Immediately they began to climb the steep slope on the other side, heading for the top of the hill, which, as Fat Rosi had informed them, was Germany. Half way up, she paused momentarily and bending down, examined the small stone which barred her way, tracing the two letters which adorned it with her plump fingers. 'B and D', she announced softly, straightening up. 'The old border till 1940. We're there. But I'll take you to the top of the hill and show you the track which leads to Bleialf, the first German village.'

'You don't need to,' Abel whispered, 'you've done enough already, Rosi, and you've got to make the long journey back alone.'

Rosi shook her fading blonde head stubbornly. 'What I set out to do, I do. I'm your guide till the top of that hill and after that you're on your own.'

'Okay, Rosi, it's up to you,' said Abel, and they set off again, panting a little as the way grew steeper.

Five minutes later, as they emerged in single file from the trees, they ran into the ambush. Dark shapes sprang up from the grass. *'Halt!'* commanded a harsh triumphant voice.

'Lauf!' Fat Rosi yelled in alarm and swung round to bolt back the way they had come.

Scarlet flame stabbed the darkness. Rosi screamed and dropped to her knees, clutching her massive bosom.

'Bastard!' Mac yelled angrily and brought up his Colt.

But as Rosi gave a last groan and slumped face downwards on the wet grass, and Cain, hidden by the trees, dived head first into the drainage ditch at the side of the track, Mac realised the hopelessness of the situation. There were at least half a dozen Germans crouching there in the grass, weapons at the alert, just waiting for an opportunity to begin the massacre. With a curse, he let his Colt drop to the ground and began to raise his hands in surrender. Behind him Abel and Spiv did the same as the alert German police advanced towards them, fingers curled around their triggers.

'Wer seid ihr?' Cain, crouched in the ditch, heard the man who had fired demand.

'Balls!' Mac growled beside himself with rage. 'Balls to you.'

'Das sind doch Englander!' another voice gasped incredulously. *'Was machen die hier?'*

Cain bit his lip angrily. The Germans knew who they were. They had been caught like a bunch of damned amateurs, right by the short and curlies. 'Blast,' he muttered under his breath and began to raise his head cautiously out of the ditch.

By the faint silver light of the stars, he viewed the scene. Fat Rosi lay sprawled carelessly in the grass in the abandoned pose of the violently done to death. His men were bunched together, obviously unnerved by the ambush. While the rest of the

Germans surrounded them, weapons at the alert, the big man who had fired first was searching the Ultra men carefully, a pistol clasped in one hand.

Cain forced himself to think. There were half a dozen Germans. If he could get close enough without being spotted, he could surprise them in turn. But how might the big German searching Abel react? Would he grab the American, thrust his pistol in his side and switch tables on the sudden intruder? It was a chance that Cain knew he couldn't take. He had to get rid of the big man first, then he could deal easily with the rest of them. He drew his knife from the side of his boot, and began to crawl forward, covered by the ditch. The twenty yards he had to cover to come round the back of the excited, triumphant Germans seemed like twenty miles. But finally he made it, his heart beating with excitement.

The big man was searching Spiv now, towering head and shoulders over the little Cockney. Cain breathed a sigh of relief. The German was just in the position he needed. It would be tricky, with the darkness and the German standing so close to Spiv. But that was a chance he would have to take. Swiftly, silently, he eased out his pistol and placed it on the top of the ditch in front of him. Then he picked up his knife again with his good hand.

He raised it behind his back and said a swift prayer. Then he flung it with all his strength. For a moment nothing happened, then the big German screamed. He flung up his hands, the hilt of the knife trembling in the small of his back, before pitching heavily on to his face.

'*Um himmelswillen–*' someone began. Cain sprang from the ditch, pistol in hand. '*Haende hoch,*' he yelled harshly. '*Wirds bald?*'

Caught by surprise, the men who had ambushed them dropped their weapons. The tables were turned.

'Well?' Cain demanded, still not taking his eyes off the line of Germans.

Slowly Spiv let the woman's head drop back into the grass. 'The poor whore's dead.'

Cain nodded. 'And the Jerry?'

Spiv moved across to the big man. With a grunt he drew out Cain's knife and wiped it across his uniform. 'Dead, sir – dead as a ruddy doornail.'

For a moment Cain considered, while both the prisoners and his own men watched him intently. From the little silver crescent shields the prisoners wore around their necks, he knew they had been ambushed not by country policemen, but by the men of the Wehrmacht's Field Gendarmerie looking, probably for deserters: headhunters, the

German soldier called them. But their reason for being there was of no importance now. What was damnably important was the fact that Ultra was in an enemy country with half a dozen enemy prisoners on their hands. What the devil was he going to do with them?

'What are your orders, Major?' Abel rose from closing Fat Rosi's eyes and folding her plump arms across her enormous bosom.

'My orders?' Cain echoed impatiently. 'These are my orders Spiv, get that dead Jerry's pistol and give it me.'

While Cain stood there rigidly, and Abel stared at him in bewilderment, Spiv brought over the pistol. Cain took it and drew out the magazine swiftly. It still contained eight 9mm slugs.

'Here,' he rapped abruptly, 'catch.'

Automatically Abel caught the pistol. 'What's this for?' he asked.

'Do I need to draw you a picture?' Cain answered. 'We're lumbered with those Jerries there. We can't take them with us, can we?'

Abel stared at him aghast, his frank eyes full of horror. 'But that would be murder – cold-blooded murder.'

'What else do you suggest we do, Captain,' Cain said coldly. 'Hand them in at the nearest German garrison and say, look what we found while we were walking through the woods.' He laughed bitterly. 'It's their lives or ours Captain Abel. What are you going to decide?'

Abel sighed and turned to face the prisoners. 'Kneel,' he ordered in German, in a voice that was strangely cracked and expressionless.

Awkwardly, the German military policemen knelt in the damp grass, their hands still clasped to their helmeted heads.

Again Abel hesitated, then slowly walked behind them. Hesitantly he clicked off the safety on the dead man's pistol. A youngster at the end of the line sobbed, and dropping his hands, turned round, his face contorted with terror to see Abel standing there, pistol in hand.

'*Bitte,*' he cried, '*bitte – nicht schiessen,*' he pleaded, tears streaming down his unlined cheeks, '*bitte!*'

Abel groaned. His grip slackened and the pistol tilted. 'I can't do it, Cain,' he cried. 'I can't just kill them – like this.'

'They killed the woman in cold blood – without warning,' Cain said, his voice low and under control. 'Pay them back for what they did to her. She was one of your common folk, wasn't she? Well, avenge her!'

Abel shook his head. 'I can't do it, Cain.'

'Och, stop blethering there like a soft great nelly!' Mac's angry voice cut in suddenly. 'If you can't do it, I bloody well will!' Swiftly he bent down and ripped the jacket off the dead man. Pushing through the kneeling policemen who had been following the exchange with tense expectancy, he grabbed the pistol out of Abel's nerveless fingers. Hastily he wrapped the weapon inside the thick jacket to muffle the explosion. Striding towards the young policeman who had cried out, he placed the muzzle against the back of his shaven skull, just behind the left ear, and pulled the trigger. There was a muffled explosion, the stink of burned flesh and the man's skull shattered in a flurry of bone and blood. The mutilated body fell to the ground, and without even waiting to draw a breath, Mac, his wrist red with blood, passed on to his next victim.

Half an hour later the massacre was over and the German headhunters, plus their guide, were hidden in the drainage ditch, covered hastily with fir branches torn off the nearest trees. Cain knew they wouldn't remain hidden there long. Hunters or a police patrol would find them after a few days. But by then, he hoped, they would have reached Trier. He hoped too that the fact they had been shot by a German weapon would conceal their role in the slaughter. Perhaps the investigators would conclude they had been killed by deserters from their own army. So they set off on the track that led to the first German village Bleialf, marching through the night in sullen silence, as if only now had they become fully aware of what they had done, and the terrible price they must pay if they were captured.

THREE

'Prum,' Cain announced, as they crouched on the height staring down at the little German town in the valley, dominated by the twin-towered cathedral, its slate roof already beginning to gleam in the slanting rays of the ascending sun. 'That road running past the Cathedral there is the main road from Aachen to Trier. You can see it, going up the hill past the railway line.'

The other three, now freshly shaven and washed with water found in a ditch beyond Bleialf, nodded.

'We could swing round the place along the heights,' Mac suggested, 'and hit the main road on that hill up there.'

He humped the pack containing his explosives a little more comfortably on his back, 'That way we could avoid the risk of meeting any nosy Jerry copper.'

'No good,' Spiv said before Cain could reply.

'What do you mean?' snapped Mac.

'Well, I know that place down there. Before the war when I was working for the Church of England–'

'The what?' Cain interrupted.

Spiv cupped his hand over his face, as if he were shielding a curved nose. 'You know, sir – C of E?'

'Oh, you mean the Jews,' Mac said.

'That's right, C of E. Well, as I was saying – and I'll try to keep it simple so that you fellers who don't understand English too well, will get me,' he cast Mac a sidelong glance, 'we used to take the people we were getting out down the main road from Aachen. But at Prum we'd get off the main road and make a beeline for the Belgie frontier over the heights and on to St Vith. But the *Grenzpolizei* got smart to us. They put one of their blokes up in that big church with a pair of binoculars, where he could watch the whole show easily. So that was the end of that particular caper and we had to find a new way across the border.'

'You mean that if they've got someone checking, it would be easiest for them to put a single chap in one of the towers, where he could easily survey the heights all around?'

'Ay, ay, Spiv, ye might be right,' Mac broke in. 'But why worry about it? So we walk through the place – instead of going round – just like a bunch of normal squareheads.'

Spiv laughed scornfully. 'Oh, yeah, you

just look like the average Jerry peasant, don't yer, with that mop of red hair of yours and a pack of bloody plastic explosive on yer back!'

Mac flushed, but before he could reply, Cain spoke. 'All right, we'll just have to take the chance of being stopped. Our *Ausweise* are first-class SOE forgeries and the rest of the documents we have are as good. But there is the problem of the language. Spiv and I can pass as Walloon volunteers working in German industry. Abel's German is excellent, so he's okay if we're stopped.' He frowned. 'You're the problem, Mac. With that red hair of yours – not very common in these parts – and not a word of German, you stick out like a sore thumb.' Cain's brow furrowed with worry. 'We'll pass through the town individually,' he said, 'and meet up again on the hill on the other side. But I think one of us must stop close to Mac, just in case he is stopped and runs into difficulties. All right,' he decided, 'Spiv you'll go in first, Mac will be next and I'll follow him close–'

'Let me cover him,' Abel broke in, speaking for the first time since he had been unable to kill the German policemen on the hill. His face was still very pale and there were dark circles under his eyes.

'You?' Cain asked hesitantly.

'Now listen, laddie,' Mac said. 'I appreciate your offer, you being the best German speaker among us. But if we get into a tight fix, there'll be no time to be standing around and examining your conscience, ye know. It'll be shoot first and ask questions later, ye ken?'

Abel nodded. 'I know that, Mac,' he said quietly but firmly. 'But still I want to go in with you.'

Cain looked at the American's determined face and remembered the scene with the unarmed combat instructor that wet morning on the heather at Special Training School Number One. 'All right, Abel, you cover Mac.'

'Thank you.'

'Okay, this is the set-up.' Swiftly Cain detailed the order in which they would enter the little town slowly coming to life below. 'But remember this,' he concluded. 'The Mission is more important than any individual one of us. If any one of us gets nabbed, that's his bad luck. The rest must go on – that includes me as well. But if anyone is captured, he *must* not talk.'

'You mean, Major, if one of us gets done, you want him to swallow the throat lozenge?'

Cain nodded. 'We all know the Gestapo. A few hours in their hands and even the toughest of us would begin to sing.' He looked at Abel pointedly. 'You all understand your responsibilities, don't you?'

'Yes,' they chorused.

'All right then, let's go.'

Slowly they worked their way down the long steep hill which ran into the little town. They all would have liked to have hurried and got through the place. But they were forced to adopt the slow measured tread of the shabbily clad peasants all around them drifting towards the market in the square opposite the Cathedral. These were country-folk who had all the time in the world. Any attempt to hurry would have aroused their suspicions.

Bringing up the rear, a dozen yards behind Mac's bulk, Abel was struck by the silence of the street. There was hardly any traffic save for a few lumbering ox-drawn carts, piled high with vegetables, obviously intended for the market, and an occasional truck belching flames from the cylindrical wood-gas producer it towed behind it as power. Otherwise the peasants said little and when they did, they spoke in whispers, as if they didn't want to be overheard by their fellows. In spite of his inner tension, Abel was surprised. Somehow he had expected the conquerors of Europe to be loud-mouthed, noisy, blustering types. These folks were exactly the opposite; timid, little, humble people.

He came to a bend in the road. A large

placard decorated the wall. Next to the sinister black figure which adorned it, the writing announced. *Ssh! The enemy is listening every where!'* Even in this remote border area, Abel told himself, they were obviously spy conscious; it was a bad sign. The great Cathedral loomed into view, its twin towers cut out like thin metal against an empty morning sky. A single bell tolled persistently. Abel wondered why. A marriage or a funeral? The worn, brick-red faces of the peasants all around him revealed nothing. Abel told himself he must concentrate on covering Mac. A skinny man in an ankle-length leather coat and with a dark felt hat pulled low over his forehead stared at the big Scot. Abel felt a twinge of fear. The man looked like every Gestapo agent he had ever seen in the movies. His fingers curled wetly over the butt of the pistol buried deep in his pocket. But next moment the thin man yawned, revealing a mouthful of gold teeth and looked away. He was harmless. Abel began to relax a little. Soon the market would swallow them up and within minutes they'd be across the railway line, hurrying up the hill to safety.

Cain had almost cleared the market full of fat women selling vegetables, squawking ducks and geese and laconic elderly farmers prodding animals with rheumaticky dirty fingers, when he spotted the cordon of policemen in green uniforms examining documents on both sides of the road beyond the market. His first instinct was to turn and mingle with the crowd of peasants again. But that might arouse suspicions. Besides there was no other way across the railway. Clenching his good hand in his trouser pocket, he felt for the hole through which he could drag up the pistol he had suspended there by a piece of string. As casually as he could he moved to the policeman on the left side of the cobbled road.

'*Ausweis,*' the policeman asked in the listless tone of the time-server, who had been asking the same question for the last twenty years.

With his hook, Cain tendered him the pass. The fat policeman glanced at it. 'Alsatian, eh,' he mused. 'Born 1910. Why aren't you in the army?' For the first time he looked up and saw Cain's hook. 'That's why. You've only got one flipper, Jean. All right, off you go.'

A minute later, Spiv came to the cordon. Whatever he might have felt inside, his face did not show; it was as cheekily cheerful as ever. '*Ausweis und Wehrpass?*' demanded the fat policeman who had stopped Cain.

Spiv cursed. SOE head office had slipped up. They had not supplied the three members of the Ultra team who were posing as German or former citizens of Alsace-

Lorraine and the East Cantons, with the *Wehrpass*. But it was too late to worry about that now. Smiling, he offered his pass, hoping his little trick from the old pre-war days of the Jewish Railway would still work.

It did. As the policeman opened the green *Ausweis*, his little, piglike eyes nearly popped from his eyes when he saw the picture of the naked girl carefully placed there, legs spread, revealing all.

'Crap on the Christmas Tree, man!' he exclaimed, breathing steamily, 'where did you get that? Oh my aching arse, look at the tits on her, will you?'

Spiv winked at him. 'Here,' he said generously, handing the fat policeman the nude photo, 'have it. It'll be something to keep you warm on a cold night.'

'Thanks,' the policeman gulped and waved Spiv on, *Wehrpass* forgotten as he goggled clammily at the naked girl's enormous swelling breasts. 'Be off with you, dirty French bastard before I have you for peddling pornography to us honest German folk comrades!'

Spiv needed no urging. The smile was still glued to his lips as he moved on, but his heart was thumping away as if it might burst his rib cage.

Mac was stopped before he had time to dodge. The wizened little policeman with the stern face and the grey toothbrush moustache trimmed in the Hitler fashion, appeared beyond the peasants leaving the market, hand held out imperiously, demanding *'Papiere!'*

A dozen paces behind Mac, Abel caught his breath and waited, still concealed by the milling crowd.

Mac's face flushed a dull red at the sight of the green German uniform and the eagle holding a swastika on the policeman's chest.

'Papiere!' the cop demanded again, rubbing his thumb and forefinger impatiently together in the German manner.

Mac looked at him blankly.

The stern look of authority in the little man's eyes disappeared to be replaced by one of genuine curiosity. *'Sind Sie kein Deutscher?'... Auslander?'*

Fervently Abel prayed that the big, red-faced Scot, who was staring down at the little cop in bull-like rage, would seize the bait offered him by the policeman and produce the papers which identified him as a Hungarian worker being transferred from Cologne to Trier to work in the war industry. But Mac did nothing of the sort. His temper got the better of him.

'What the hell are you standing there for, man?' he yelled 'Jawing at me in that lingo of yours like I was some bloody Jerry?'

'Englander!' the little cop cried in both

100

alarm and surprise. *'Wachmeister, ich hab' einen Tommy erwischt!'*

Just as Mac tried to pull out his pistol, Abel threw himself into his back and hissed, 'For Christ's sake, don't draw that gun! Leave this to me!' Without waiting for Mac's reaction, he blundered past him and yelled at the surprised cop in German, 'Yes, yes, don't shoot. We're Tommies... Escaped prisoners-of-war.' His face contorted with apparent fear, he raised his hands high in the air, *'Don't shoot, POWs!'*

Suddenly the two of them were surrounded by excited cops and gawping, chattering peasants, whose animated faces showed they'd never experienced a market day like this one before. Big hands ran the length of their bodies. Their passes were seized and examined with a great deal of lip-smacking and half-admiring cries of *'wunderbare Arbeit ... absolut echt'*, while Abel nodded his head urgently, assuring the cops they had been forged in the Stalag.

Then the little cop with the wizened face and the Hitler-moustache discovered Mac's pistol. *'Pistole,'* he yelled and brandished it in front of his colleagues. *'Der Tommy hat eine Pistole, Herr Wachmeister!'*

Swiftly the Sergeant in charge, who was wearing some sort of riding boots and ill-fitting breeches, ordered that Abel should be searched for arms too. His pistol was found moments later and brandished to the awed, excited crowd.

That did it. The middle-aged cops fell back a pace, pistols levelled at their two prisoners, as if they were wild men who might run amok at any moment. Behind them the suddenly scared peasants tried to get out of the way, especially when Mac lowered his brick-red head like a bull about to charge. For one crazy moment Abel felt he was going to laugh out loud at the sheer stupidity of the whole scene: the terrified peasants; the self-important Police Sergeant, who was now mounting a rusty bicycle, his leather breeches threatening to split at any moment; Mac looking like the traditional bull in a china shop. It was all too much like something out of a pre-war Hollywood B-movie. But the sudden hard nudge of a pistol muzzle in the small of his back told him that this was for real.

With the fat Sergeant wobbling unsteadily at their head on his cycle, their suspicious guards, hands clasping their pistols tightly on both sides, and the awed, fearful peasants following at a respectful distance, they started to march towards the local jail and the punishment which waited for them there.

FOUR

'Shit, shit, shit!' Cain cursed and slashed his hook viciously against the trunk of the nearest tree. 'That damned Scots man!'

Spiv shrugged carelessly, as they stood there on the hillside on the other side of Prum, watching the little procession of prisoners and policemen disappear from sight down a little alley. 'What do you expect, Major – a great ugly Jock who goes at things like a bull at a gate and a Yank who hasn't got his knees brown yet?'

Cain hardly heard him. Somehow or other he knew he could trust the two of them; they wouldn't talk. They'd take the L-tablet when the pressure got too much. Yet he knew he couldn't sacrifice them without making some attempt to save them.

'You know what you said, Major,' Spiv said suddenly, apparently reading his mind. 'The mission is more important than any individual one of us. Shall we sling our hook while the going's good?'

'No,' Cain snapped firmly. 'We won't sling our hook. We're going to give them a chance.'

'How do you mean, sir?'

'Well, Spiv, my guess is that that lot of country bobbies down there won't get anything out of Mac and Captain Abel.'

'Yeah, you're right there,' Spiv agreed. 'Your average Jerry rozzer is all talk, in my experience. They might give you a couple of clouts over the head if yer cheeky. But otherwise they're harmless enough.'

'That's my opinion too, Spiv. They'll simply put the two of them in the lock-up and wait till the Gestapo come to fetch them – they'll have found their pistols by now of course – and let the heavies do the questioning. So the question is how long will it take for the heavies in the long leather coats to arrive? Where's the nearest Gestapo post?'

Spiv considered for a moment. 'You can take your pick, Major. Malmedy, Aachen, Cologne, perhaps Trier.'

Cain did a quick calculation. 'All of them between eighty and a hundred kilometres from Prum,' he announced after a moment. 'So with the way these Eifel roads are, it could take them anything between two and three hours to get here.'

'Right, sir. But what are you getting at?'

'Getting at?' Cain echoed. 'Why, that'll give us two to three hours to get them out.'

'But what about the throat lozenges and all that?'

Cain's reply was a single, harsh 'Balls!'

'Now listen, Mac,' Abel whispered urgently, as the Sergeant with ill-cut leather breeches dismounted from his bike and ponderously opened the door to the little jail, 'we're sunk once they find that explosive. So far, I've convinced them we're escaped POWs, with faked papers. The pistols we pinched somewhere during our escape. But if they find that plastic, we've really had it.'

'Ay, ay,' Mac agreed, speaking from the side of his mouth, while the Sergeant still stamped his feet and adjusted his breeches, 'but what we gonna do?'

'This. It's dangerous, but it's the only way–'

They had just begun their search of the two prisoners in the little nineteenth-century jail which stank of sweat, stale white cabbage and human misery, when Mac did it. As the little cop with the Hitler moustache turned his attention from a pale-faced Abel to him, he ripped the L-tablet from its hiding place behind his lapel and held it up high, as if undecided. Then he cried out loud and thrust it into his wide open mouth.

Instinctively the Sergeant seemed to realise what the tablet contained. 'Stop him,' he yelled urgently, swinging his polished boots from the desk where he had been resting them, 'Stop him, Heinz! The Tommy's trying to poison himself!'

'Yes, poison,' Abel added his cry to the Sergeant's. 'In the camp they gave him cyanide!'

The little cop lunged at Mac. The Scot fended him off with a blow to the chest. As the cop staggered back, Mac seemed to make one final decision. He swallowed the tablet. Together the little cop and the Sergeant threw themselves on him as he sank to the floor. They forced open his throat. It was empty. But there was the telltale blue stain of cyanide on his tongue.

For a moment the two Germans stared down at him paralysed and uncertain, as their prisoner looked up at them in numb expectancy. Then the Sergeant broke the spell.

'Get on to the hospital at Bitburg,' he cried urgently. 'Tell them! No better, see if Doctor Schmittheim has a stomach pump! Anything that'll clear the fool's stomach.'

'It's no good,' Abel said sadly, his eyes brimming with sudden tears, as he looked down at his dying companion. 'Can't you see? It's acting already. They said at the camp it would be all over in a matter of seconds.'

Aghast, the cops watched while the big Scot's face flushed an ugly crimson as he lay there on the stone floor. His thick fingers clutched at his throat. It almost seemed as if he were trying to strangle himself, as he writhed back and forth on the floor, his knees tucked into his stomach, fighting desperately for breath. Suddenly he straightened out, his spine arched and taut like a bow. He gasped and his head fell to one side, eyes staring into nothing.

The little cop darted forward, but Abel was quicker. 'Let me,' he cried fervently. 'He was my comrade!'

Abel knelt beside the prostrate Scot and lowered his head to his chest. The cops held their breath, as he knelt there thus for what seemed a long time. Slowly Abel turned and looked at them, tears streaming down his ashen cheeks. He shook his head wordlessly. Then he reached forward and with gentle fingers, closed the dead man's eyes.

'Well?' Cain demanded under his breath, as Spiv returned to their observation post, in the cobbled alley opposite the little jail.

'Four rozzers in the outer office and a couple more inside, as far as I can judge. But I can't say with certainty, sir.'

'Hm, six of them. I suppose we could tackle them, eh, Spiv? We'd have surprise on our side.'

'Come off it, sir,' Spiv said scornfully. 'Breaking into a Jerry jail in broad daylight in the middle of a town! Christ, we'd have the whole bloody lot of them after us. Then we'd really be up the creek without the proverbial paddle!'

Cain knew the little Cockney was right. If it were dark, they would have a chance. But not in broad daylight. He flashed a glance down at his wristwatch. It was already over an hour since they had arrested Mac and Abel. They didn't have much time left before the Gestapo arrived.

The same thought was going through Abel's mind as he sat facing the Sergeant and the little man across the bare wooden table, drinking his fifth schnapps since Mac had committed suicide. His appeal to the inherent German sentimentality that contrasts so strongly with their cruelty had worked.

Even the little cop with the Hitler moustache had felt for him after the Scot's death; he had clapped Abel on the back and muttered, 'Don't take it so hard, Tommy. Perhaps he's better off there' – he indicated Mac's body which they had placed reverently in an empty cell, pack still on his back – 'than where you're going soon.' And the Sergeant had fetched a big stone bottle of corn schnapps from a cupboard and had insisted he should drink a glass 'to get over it'.

One drink had led to another. As the fat Sergeant had rumbled, his face already beginning to flush crimson, 'A man can't stand on one leg, Tommy, you'd better have another!'

Now the alcohol was having its effect and the barriers were down. The fat Sergeant, his tunic ripped open, beads of sweat rolling down his cheeks, kept repeating, 'Of course, we old ones didn't want the war. After all we fought in the first lot, didn't we Heinz? We know what war's like.'

'Yes, yes,' the little cop had repeated dutifully, 'we who were at Verdun know what war's like all right.'

After his fourth *Korn*, Abel had ventured to ask where they were going to send him. In reply the little cop, now relaxed and no longer stern, had pressed his arm warmly and said, 'Don't worry Tommy, we'll put in a good word for you when they come to pick you up. We Germans and you Tommies should never have fought against each other in the first place. Now if we'd have tackled the Ivans...'

It was only after his fifth drink of the fiery spirit that Abel had felt it was again opportune to ask them where he was to be sent and the Sergeant's drunken answer sent a shiver of fear down his spine. 'To Aachen Gestapo HQ for questioning.' He dabbed his dripping brow with a flowered handkerchief. 'You see it's because of the cannons' – he meant the pistols – 'they want to talk to you about them. But don't worry, Tommy, we'll see you're all right.'

While the two cops downed their fifth

Korn and the Sergeant began to fill the glasses with a hand that trembled violently, Abel did the same calculation as Cain had done and came to the same conclusion: time was running out fast.

Feigning drunkenness, he staggered to his feet suddenly, almost upsetting his glass, 'Must urinate,' he announced, 'where's the bucket.'

The fat Sergeant grinned. '*Ja*, it certainly goes through a man doesn't it?' he agreed. 'All right, Heinz, show the Tommy where the piss corner is.'

Together they staggered out past the unlocked cell where Mac lay on the floor, his body rigid. Abel looked down at him anxiously. The little cop reached up and patted him sympathetically on the shoulder, as if he could guess what was going through the pale-faced Tommy's mind.

'Don't think about it, son,' he said, his speech slurred. 'We've all got to go at one time or another. Now get yer flies undone and get on with it so we can have another snort before the Gestapo arrives. There's the piss corner.'

Fumbling with his flies, Abel stood legs apart at the evil-smelling, black-painted wall, his mind racing. Had he made a terrible mistake? Had he given Mac the wrong dope after all? God, it didn't bear thinking about!

Opening his mouth, he began to bawl to the tune of the current Vera Lynn favourite *'Now is the Hour:* now is the time ... for all good men ... to come to the aid of the party ... *now...'*

'What are you singing for?' the little cop asked. 'Have you no respect for your dead comrade, Tommy, singing like that while yer standing there pissing?'

Abel finished and fumbled with his flies again. 'It was his favourite tune,' he said thickly, a mournful look on his pale face. 'I thought I'd sing to him for one last time before they take me away.'

Genuine tears started into the little cop's eyes. 'You're a good pal,' he said, and dug his knuckles into his eyes to drive back the tears. At that moment, Mac lying stiffly on the floor winked solemnly at Abel. He had got the message.

Abel was happily drinking his sixth schnapps, relieved that by swallowing instead of crunching the tablet Mac had come to no harm, when suddenly the door was flung open and Mac was standing there, hamlike fists doubled, a grin of anticipation on his broad ugly face.

The little cop swung round. His mouth dropped open stupidly.

Mac hit him. Not very hard. But the blow sufficed. The little cop sailed over the back of his chair and sprawled full length on the floor. He was unconscious before he even struck it.

On the other side of the room, the fat Sergeant struggled for his pistol. Mac lunged forward. With a grunt, he lifted the Sergeant clean out of his seat, struggling and cursing in red-faced impotence. The Sergeant bellowed as he hit the floor on his schnapps-filled belly. Mac grinned maliciously. He could not resist the target. 'Let's see if I can get a goal with this one, Yank.' Drawing back his big boot, he launched a mighty kick at the Sergeant's rump. He shot forward, as if propelled by a rocket and slammed into the other wall. He gave one sad gasp like a punctured balloon, and collapsed.

'Goal!' cried the big Scot.

Abel held his finger to his lips for silence and then shook him enthusiastically by the hand. 'Thank God, you're all right, Mac. If you only knew how I felt when I saw you swallow that L-tablet!'

Mac grinned and wiped the sweat off his face. 'How do you think I felt!' He breathed out hard. 'But you did a pretty good job of play acting yourself, man. God, how you greeted!'

'You mean the crying bit, Mac? I was the leading light of the Princeton Dramatic Society. But come on, we can't stand here chatting. The Gestapo is on its way to pick us up.'

Mac hesitated. 'What about them?' he asked, pointing to Abel's drinking companions. 'We can't just leave them here just like that. They'd have the whole damn countryside on our back as soon as they came to again.'

'Yeah, Mac, I know that. But what can we do? If we kill them, we'll still be in the same fix. Those guys out there in the other office know we're English. They'll come gunning for us too – but with a vengeance. Don't think I'm trying to chicken out, Mac–'

Mac held up his hand for silence, his brow creased with thought. 'Ay you're right there, man,' he said after a moment. 'Either way they'd have us by the short hairs. But what can we do?'

'Listen Mac, do you think you could fake up something with those fireworks of yours in the pack,' he asked. 'Something like a bomb?'

'Yes, why?'

'Look at this.' Abel pointed to the handle behind the sergeant's desk. 'It's to sound the air-raid siren on the roof. If we sounded it, with a bit of luck, we'd have the bunch of them outside running for the nearest shelter and most of the local yokels too so the streets would be cleared. Then you could fake your bomb.'

Understanding dawned on the Scot's face.

113

'Ay, it sounds a right bonny scheme. Well, come on, laddie, don't just stand there – give me a hand with this here plastic explosive.'

For the next five minutes Mac worked feverishly, while Abel watched the door anxiously, knowing they had only a matter of minutes left now before the Gestapo arrived. He kneaded the plastic explosive, which filled the room with the heavy sickly smell of almonds, into a ball and then thrust a small metal device into it.

'A pull switch,' he explained, attaching a long line of string to the device. 'And I've got enough band here to explode the plastic from outside yon door there.' Swiftly he cast around for somewhere to plant the home-made bomb to give the maximum effect. Then he spotted what he wanted – an ancient pot-bellied stove, obviously used to heat the room in winter. He opened the door and carefully placed the explosive inside it. He began to play out the line until it reached the door.

For a moment he stood there eyeing the scene with a professional eye. Finally he said: 'We'll need them closer to the stove, Yank, if we want to have the bomb effect.'

Abel looked down at the two elderly policemen and hesitated. They had treated him well enough; they weren't bad men, just time-servers who had carried out their

114

duties as they saw them. Yet now they had to die.

'Well?' Mac demanded. 'Let's move it, Yank. We haven't got all day.'

'Of course. Let's take the fat Sergeant first.'

Swiftly the two unconscious policemen were placed with their heads close to the stove so that the explosion would kill them instantly.

Satisfied, Mac threw a last eye around the room. 'Looks all right to me, Yank,' he said. 'All right, get ready with that siren.'

Trying not to look at the two cops, who had shared their schnapps with him and would never wake up again, Abel started to whirl the handle behind the desk. The high-pitched howl of the German siren killed the silence. For a moment nothing happened and then suddenly there was the sound of feet hurrying purposefully down the cobbled alley outside. There were shouts of alarm and fear. Somewhere on the other side of the valley in which Prum lay, another siren took up the howl.

Mac looked at Abel in triumph. 'They've bought it, laddie,' he hissed. 'Bought it, hook, line and sinker.'

'Give them another couple of minutes, then we'll slip out.'

Tensely the two Ultra men waited till the hurrying sound outside started to die away.

Abel took one last glance at the two still bodies.

'Okay, Mac, let's go.'

Mac needed no urging. He thrust his pistol into his belt and made for the door. Abel followed him. One of the cops groaned and began to stir. But Abel didn't look back. He slammed the door behind him and ran towards the other side of the alley where Mac was already crouched, big hand tensed on the string.

'Watch yer ruddy head,' he hissed, 'here we go!'

Just as Cain and Spiv sidled into view, pistols at the ready, the big Scot tugged the string and the little room across the way erupted in a thick choking crump.

FIVE

Oberkommissar Kranz of the *Geheime Staatspolizei* looked around the shattered room in silence, the unlit stump of a ten-pfennig cigar glued to his thick, wet bottom lip. Without removing it, he turned to the policeman to whom Spiv had given the picture of the naked girl, and asked, 'Which was your Sergeant?'

The policeman licked his dry lips. 'That

one,' he whispered, 'the one without the head.'

'Hm.'

For what seemed an age the Gestapo man stood, staring at the headless body, in his long ankle-length leather coat which creaked audibly with every breath, sucking at the cold cigar. Then he began to speak, slowly and carefully with a clear pause after each phrase, as if he were used to dealing with fools or those who were so scared that they couldn't think straight any more, 'So the siren sounded... You all ran for the air-raid shelter... A few minutes later you heard the bomb explode... When no all clear had sounded after an hour, you came out of the shelter ... and found this... Correct?'

'Correct.'

Outside someone was sweeping away broken glass with a broom, whistling tunelessly as he did so. Kranz frowned. The whistling seemed out of place. But he dismissed it from his mind and concentrated on his problem, while the cop stared at him, thinking that with his slanting deep-set eyes, the Gestapo man looked a sly one. Kranz caught the look and smiled to himself, a little pleased. He was proud of his eyes, which had gained him the nickname of *der Schlaue,* even though he himself knew that he was not cunning; his success had always been achieved by dogged, persistent policework; by not giving up when his colleagues had long thrown in the towel.

'Do you know,' Kranz said suddenly in an almost conversational tone, 'that Air District Five HQ ... reports there has been no enemy air activity ... over South-West Germany ... since six o'clock this morning?'

'But the bomb, *Herr Kommissar* – and,' he indicated the headless corpse sprawled out in the corner like a broken doll.

'Yes the bomb.' Kranz smiled, but the slanting eyes remained cold and without expression. 'Funny weapon that ... must be a new kind of selective bomb.'

The fat policeman looked at him, as if he had suddenly gone crazy. 'What Commissar?'

'Yes, it can pick out the nationalities ... it wants to kill... It only kills Germans, you see ... *not Tommies!*' Kranz thrust out his thick bottom lip with the cigar still stuck to it. 'Funny, eh?'

'I see what you mean, Commissar. Why weren't the Tommies killed with the poor old Sarge and Heinz?' He warmed to the subject, 'and where are the Tommies anyway?'

'Exactly,' Kranz agreed. 'Now tell me ... a little more about ... those two Tommies of yours.'

The fat cop told him what he knew; once again, Kranz went into one of his brooding silences, absorbing the information, worrying it like a dog a bone, kicking it around his brain, trying to give it some shape, form it into a recognisable pattern. 'Two Englishmen,' he mused aloud, 'with good identity documents ... one of them speaking fluent German ... and both armed with pistols... And you believed that they'd escaped from some POW camp or other.' He sniffed delicately, the cigar jerking up and down on his bottom lip. 'Some folk would believe in Father Christmas, if they weren't told different... Do you know what I think?'

'No, *Herr Kommissar?*'

'I think you country flatfoots ... stumbled on to something big ... something very big.' For the first time since he had entered the wrecked police station, he took the cold cigar out of his mouth and barked, his voice no longer measured, and soft, but harsh and urgent. 'And I think we'd better get on to HQ and have them sound a security alert, stage one for the whole of the Eifel. *Now...*'

They lay tense and stiff in the thick undergrowth of the pine forest which bordered the highway to Bitburg and listened to the drone of the motor fading into the distance. Mac moved, as if he were about to raise his head above the bushes, but Cain hissed at him urgently to keep down. Whoever was looking for them on the road – and there was no doubt now that Ultra was being searched for – might be travelling in pairs at intervals. He forced himself to count to sixty; then he raised his head cautiously. The cobbled highway which wound through the valleys from Prum to Bitburg was empty.

'All right,' he whispered softly, 'you can sit up now and remember, no noise. Sound carries a long way on hot afternoons like these.'

'Hot,' Spiv sat up and wiped the sweat off his smart Cockney face, 'you can say that again, Major. It's like a bloody bakehouse oven!'

'Ye get your share of it,' Mac growled unsympathetically. He was still wearing his pack, as if he could not bear to be parted from his precious explosives.

'Well,' Cain said softly, 'I think we can safely assume now that they're on to us. That was a damn fine scheme of yours Abel – and it saved old Mac's bacon for him – but I'm afraid it didn't work. They're out looking for us – at least you two – in full strength.'

'What are we going to do, Cain?' Abel asked, miserable that in spite of the fact that he had sacrificed the two policemen, his ruse had not paid off.

'Well, for a start we can't stay here. Listen.' He cocked his head to one side so that he could hear better and the others followed suit. From far away there came the sound of harsh male voices and the barking of dogs. 'A search party,' Cain commented tonelessly.

'Ay, they'll be the beaters all right,' Mac agreed.

'What do you bloody-well think we are, Mac,' Spiv said angrily. 'Ruddy foxes or something!'

'That is exactly what we are,' Cain said calmly. 'And if you remember rightly – foxes are very smart animals. So we've got to – I hope you'll forgive the pun – outfox them. For a start then, we don't hole up till nightfall, as they probably expect us to do. We keep on going during daylight. Now obviously we can't walk along the heights.' He indicated the bare hilltops on both sides. 'We'd be too visible on the skyline. So where would they expect us to hide out? Right here where we are at this moment – in the forest. Okay, now let them wear themselves out, beating the trees. We're going to take the easy way down to Trier.'

'What do you mean?' Abel asked.

'We're going to take the road.'

'That's ruddy chancy, Major!' Spiv protested.

'I know – that's why we're going to take it. Look, the trees on both sides should cover us pretty effectively from the air and to make doubly sure, we're all going to pick up one of those planks over there,' he indicated the neat heap of one-metre-long pine planks at the edge of the forest, 'and carry it on our shoulders. From the air we'll look like workers. We use the road, strung out at fifty-feet intervals, sticking close to the ditch. As soon as you hear a motor, into it and lie doggo; you can assume that any motor traffic in these parts is out looking for us. Now I'll bring up the rear in case there's any trouble.'

'And who'll take the lead?' Abel asked.

Cain looked at him directly, his eyes searching the American's sun-flushed face. 'You, Abel. You're our German linguist. You can give us the wire if you spot trouble – a village, a patrol or anything like that. Okay?'

'Okay,' Abel replied with the same carelessness Cain had used, yet at that moment his heart began to beat a little faster. By giving him the point, Cain had accepted him at last, warts and all. He was part of the team.

All that long afternoon, the Ultra men plodded steadily southwards down the blindingly white, dusty road, praying for the moment when the yellow ball of the sun would finally sink beyond the parched green of the hills and allow them to sink down and rest. Twice *Opel Blitz* trucks, filled with helmeted soldiers, came crawling along the highway, the soldiers peering suspiciously to both sides. But both times they were quicker and had concealed themselves in the stinking, nettle-filled ditch before the trucks had come round the bend. Once a Fiesler Storch spotting plane had come zooming in low from behind the nearest hill, the glass of its cockpit sparkling in the sunshine. For a moment Cain had almost panicked. The plane had caught him completely off guard. But he prevented himself from bolting for the trees. Instead, he paused in the middle of the road and lowering the plank slowly like a countryman who had all the time in the world, waved at the pilot. The pilot had waved back and flown on.

Now it was nearly evening, the air beginning to cool off at last and the sun was already poised on the edge of the hills, as if it could not quite decide whether or not to slip from view for another day. Long black shadows were sliding cautiously down the valley. In another half hour it would be dark. Cain decided to call a halt.

'All right,' he ordered softly. 'Fall out into the trees. Mac you take the first stage. I'll relieve you in fifteen minutes. Okay, move it.'

They needed no urging. They staggered from the road and blundering their way through the trees, dropped wearily into the blessed relief of the cool bushes. For what seemed an age, no one spoke, no one moved, save Mac who surveyed the road carefully, his face brick-red, his big nose already beginning to peel with sunburn. Finally Cain sighed and sat up again. His feet felt as if he had been walking for weeks. 'Okay,' he said hoarsely, 'you can break open your escape kits now and see what Baker Street has provided us with in the way of food.'

The other three reached in their shabby jackets and tugged at the loose thread they found there. The lining came away to reveal a narrow package wrapped in waxed cloth. Fumbling with clumsy, heat-thickened fingers, they began to unwrap it.

'Keep your eyes front,' Cain commanded, and examined the contents of his package: an empty water bottle of thin rubber, which looked like a purse his grandmother might have used; a bar of bitter chocolate, already going white with age; a book of matches; chewing gum; Horlicks tablets and some cakes of concentrated food.

'Bloody hell,' Spiv commented, spreading his on the parched grass in front of him, 'what a feast to set before a king! Horlicks and dried pemmican – I can't wait to sink my choppers into such delicacies! Swop my gum for your choco, eh, Yank?'

'Heaven, arse and twine, Major!' Kranz exploded, the cigar stump moving up and down with his bottom lip like a yo-yo, 'haven't you found them yet?'

The young Major, with the black patch

over his left eye and the Wound Medal in Silver on his chest, flushed at the Gestapo man's outburst. 'No, *Herr Kommissar*,' he rapped, trying to contain his temper. 'What can you expect from a reserve battalion, made up of cripples like myself! This Eifel country is rough, and they could be anywhere too. Some of my men have only been out of hospital a couple of weeks, you remember.'

Kranz pulled himself together and nodded. 'It's been a long day,' he said more calmly, 'and very hot... Please excuse me.'

'You're excused,' the one-eyed veteran of Russia said coldly. 'But what are your orders now, *Herr Kommissar?*'

Kranz went into one of his long silences while he pondered. By now he was fully convinced the two missing Englishmen were not escaped POWs. The HQ of the POW organisation had confirmed that no British prisoners were missing. Besides if they had been, they surely would have headed into Belgium, rather than deeper into Germany, as all the signs indicated they were now doing. So, there were two questions that must be answered: one, what was their mission – and he was sure that they had some mission within the Reich; two, what was their destination?

'Let us have a look ... at the map,' Kranz said.

Together the two men pored over the road system leading out of Prum. 'Forget the roads into Belgium,' Kranz said slowly, 'let's concentrate on the roads leading into the Reich.'

'The road to Gerolstein and on to Koblenz is out,' the young Major said decisively, stabbing the map with his forefinger. 'The Second Armoured Division is holding a scheme all over that area. Nearly fifteen thousand troops and a couple of hundred vehicles are involved. They're as thick as fleas on the ground there – your two Tommies couldn't possibly slip through them.'

'And the road back to Aachen is out, too,' Kranz said. 'It would have been impossible for them to get through there... It must be here ... the road to Bitburg, Major.'

'But my bunch of cripples have searched the area all afternoon with a fine tooth-comb. We even had a *Storch* up.'

It was the sort of excuse for failure Kranz had been hearing all his professional life; people simply gave up too easily. But Konrad Kranz didn't; that was why he was a senior commissar and not a flatfoot pounding a beat in Berlin-Wedding today. As the yellow ball of the sun finally slipped beyond the Eifel hills and the creaking ancient waiters in the *Hotel Prumerhof* in which he had established his HQ that afternoon, started to put up the blackout,

Kranz said softly, 'Well, Major, you'd better search it again, eh?'

It was neither a request nor an order, but a threat. The young Major who had gone through the horror of the Russian winter of 1941, stared at those cunning eyes and shuddered. They were the fathomless eyes of a sadist.

SIX

'I paid sixpence to see
A tattooed Scotch lady,
She was a sight to see.
Tattooed from head to knee–'

Spiv sang the bawdy song tonelessly and interminably as they marched across the black Eifel countryside, while Abel limped after him and Mac, too worn to keep his monocle screwed in his eye, blundered blindly after the American.

'Under her jaw
Was the Royal Flying Corps
And on her back
Was the Union Jack
What could you ask for more?
Up and down her spine

127

Were the King's Own Guards in line
And right around her hips
Was a fleet of battleships—'

'How's it going, Abel?' Cain asked, drawing level with the limping American.

'Just a slight case of athlete's foot, Major,' Abel cracked wearily. 'But I'm off the critical list.'

Cain chuckled. 'Good for you, Abel.'

He passed on and took the lead again. The boys were bearing up very well after a night when the pursuit had not let up for a minute. Now it was nearly dawn and soon, he knew, he must let them rest. For since midnight when they had been surprised on the Bitburg road by a group of German soldiers who had approached virtually noiselessly on bicycles, they had been going across country, getting ever further away from their objective.

At about three he had tried to double back to the Bitburg-Trier road. But they hadn't gone far when they had heard faint shouts and the sound of men beating bushes and grass aside with sticks. They had dropped to the earth immediately, and sure enough, a long line of black silhouettes had come over the skyline, working their way slowly but purposefully towards them. And that had been that. They turned and fled into the unknown once again.

Now Cain, preoccupied with the problem of finding a resting place for his men, suddenly smelled water. He knew he wasn't mistaken; it was a gift of his. Somewhere close by there was a large body of water, a lake or river perhaps. Cain tried to remember the rivers that ran through the area. It couldn't be the Kyll or the Salm – they ran from west to east – and this smell was coming from the north.

Cain quickened his pace. Once he had orientated himself, he would be in a better position to decide where they might hide during the daylight hours. With a groan, Spiv launched into yet another version of the *Tattooed Scotch Lady:*

'Over her kidney
Was a bird's eye view of Sydney
But what I liked best
Upon her chest
Was my home in Tennessee!'

while the others stumbled after him in silence.

Dawn came swiftly, flooding the empty countryside. Cain quickened the pace even more. Behind him the other three stumbled across a road and into the fields on the other side like blind men, in their exhaustion making as much noise as a herd of cows. But Cain knew there would be no stopping until he found out where they damn well were.

Suddenly they breasted a height and found themselves on the skyline. Down below Cain caught a glimpse of the silver snake of a great river. But he had no time to examine it; they were dangerously outlined on the skyline.

'Down,' he hissed, 'get down at once!'

They flopped urgently into the nearest ditch with a sigh of relief. For a few moments Cain let them rest there, eyes closed in exhaustion, chests heaving. There was no sound save the call of a lark and the crunch of the cows a few yards away tearing at the lush, dawn-damp summer grass.

Finally Cain raised himself to his knees and stared down at the river far down below, set between the serrated terraces of its banks. Spiv was the first to join him.

'Do you know where we are, Major?' he asked, his voice husky and strained.

'I think so and we're a damned long way off our objective,' Cain answered slowly, running his gaze up and down the winding valley.

'What is it then?' Mac demanded grumpily.

'The River Moselle, if I'm not mistaken. None of the other Eifel rivers can take barges like those,' he indicated the tiny boats moving sluggishly along the silver snake, 'and those plants are grape vines. You won't find those on the Rivers Salm and Kyll.' He paused. 'But where the hell we are on the Moselle between Koblenz and Trier is completely beyond me, I'm afraid.'

'Well, there's one way to find out,' Abel said thickly.

'Yeah,' Spiv said contemptuously, 'go down there and ask one of the local yokels and get our arses kicked into the nearest nick by the Jerry rozzers!'

'No,' Abel replied politely, 'not exactly. You see on the Moselle, they're very proud of their wines. So wherever you get a good vintage, the owner will paint the name of the vintage in large letters on one of those rock outcrops you can see everywhere. For instance, *Wehlener Sonnenuhr or Trittenheimer–*'

'Spare us the lecture, Professor,' Cain cut in drily. 'We've got the big picture. Come on, let's get down there among the vines before it gets too light and see what we can find out...'

Cain didn't see the file of drab, kerchiefed girls, plodding stolidly and in silence up the steep trail between the tall vines, heavy wicker-work baskets on their bent shoulders, until it was too late. By then he knew he couldn't turn back. Besides, the others were at his heels and in their present state of near exhaustion, they would not have reacted quickly enough. Cursing at his lack of foresight, he continued down the path to meet them, head lowered, conscious of their suddenly curious gaze as the two groups approached each other. As the Ultra team came level with them, the girls stood to one side to let them pass, their flat, hard-working faces blank.

Cain forced a smile. *'Danke – Gruss Gott!'* he said in his best Bavarian-German, learnt in Munich in 1938 in preparation for the Army Interpreter's Exam.

The girls didn't reply, but as soon as they were out of earshot, Abel whispered urgently. 'You just blued it, Major.'

'What do you mean?'

'That *Gruss Gott* stands out a mile. They don't use that phrase as a greeting around here.'

'All right, all right,' Cain said, angry with Abel, with himself and the damnfool women who had appeared from nowhere, 'don't come the schoolmaster on me. Let's get the hell out of here, before they raise the alarm!'

But already it was too late. Just as they turned round the next bend, half a dozen female voices cried, hesitant at first, but more determined a moment later: 'They're over here!'

'Where?' a harsh male voice floated down from the heights above them. Cain spun round and stared through the tall vines.

The skyline was jagged with the helmeted heads of their pursuers.

'Come on,' he cried urgently. 'The buggers are right behind us!'

'Down here!' the girls screamed shrilly, 'down here among the vines!'

'We're coming in!' called the harsh soldier's voice, and as the Ultra men began to blunder wildly through the tall vines, slithering down the steep slope in a cloud of dust and slate chippings, urgent whistles sounded above them. The soldiers moved over the edge of the hill, rifles at the ready.

Cain and the others reached the bottom of the slope. Cain flung a wild look over his shoulder. They had perhaps a hundred and fifty yards lead on the Germans. But now he could see that the long line of their pursuers was spreading out, curving in at both ends as it approached the cobbled road running along the bank of the Moselle. It was obvious that the Germans were trying to cut them off.

'This way,' he yelled. 'For Chrissake – at the double!'

Swiftly he pelted down a cinder track towards a low tumbled-down farmhouse. He vaulted a gate. Mac blundered into it. 'Get rid of that damn pack!' he bellowed. Mac did so and jumped after the rest.

The cries of the Germans were getting louder. Whistles shrilled. Someone yelled in hoarse triumph, 'They're down by the farm!'

Cain pounded down a muddy track, then suddenly skidded to a halt. A man was standing in the middle of the track, legs apart, shotgun grasped in his big hands. 'Duck!' Cain screamed.

The farmer pulled the trigger of his shotgun. It erupted in a blast of scarlet flame. Pellets whizzed through the air viciously. Mac yelped with pain, as a couple of them struck him. Behind Cain, Spiv fired instinctively. Cain felt the flame sear his right side. The farmer threw up his arms and screamed, his face a bloody pulp.

But he had served his purpose. He had held them up. Dark grey figures were already bursting from the vines ahead. Their path was blocked. 'Back the way we came,' Cain gasped. 'Come on – get your fingers out!'

They swung round and pelted along the cinder track. A farmhand, naked to the waist, tried to bar Cain's way. Without even stopping, Cain raked the man's bare chest with his hook. Cain sprang over his writhing body and ran on. The others followed.

Behind them the sounds of the pursuit were growing louder. Cain spurted, forgetting his exhaustion in the urgency of the chase. The first house of the little waterside village loomed up. Everywhere the village dogs were beginning to bark frantically. Cain skidded to a halt. Up ahead, the cobbled, manure-stained narrow village road divided into two forks. Which should he take?

His mind was made up for him by the sound of heavy hobnailed boots pounding down the road to the left. 'Take the right fork,' he gasped. 'Move it!'

A cart filled with empty wine barrels barred the way. Mac raised his boot. His size eleven crashed into the cart's ancient wheel. The wood splintered easily. The cart lurched to one side and the barrels began to roll down the road. They sprang over them. Not so their pursuers. Suddenly the air was filled with angry curses as the Germans went sprawling full length over the unexpected obstacles.

Still running, Cain breathed out a fervent sigh of relief. The barrels had saved their bacon – for a minute or two at least. They pelted on down the road, the sound of their boots on the stained cobbles echoing and re-echoing in the narrow chasm of a street. But the shutters which barred the windows of the white-painted houses on both sides remained obstinately unopened, as if the occupants were crouched there fearfully, not daring to face the strange danger which had erupted so abruptly in their peaceful village.

Panting wildly, their faces grotesquely

contorted and lathered in sweat, they swung round a corner. The Moselle lay before them.

'The river!' Abel gasped, his chest heaving frantically, as they came to a halt.

Spiv's mouth dropped open. 'Christ, I can't swim *that!*'

Cain took in the situation at a glance. 'No, none of us could … the current's too swift… We'd never make it!'

'What are we going to do?' Mac asked. 'Come on make yer bloody mind up, Cain. Yon Jerries are nearly on us now.'

The Scot was right. The sound of the pursuit was coming close again. Cain could hear the officers and NCOs rapping out their orders. They were hemmed in between the village and the river.

Wildly he cast around for some means of escape. Then he saw his way out. 'The bridge,' he yelled suddenly, 'on to the bridge.'

'But there are blokes on the other side,' Spiv objected, 'Jerries!'

'Don't worry. Do as I say!'

'*Hier druben,*' a triumphant voice shouted, not fifty yards behind them, but with its owner still out of sight, '*sie sind hier langs gegangen!*'

It spurred them into action. Blindly they ran towards the iron bridge. Below lay the river, broad, cold and deep. On the other side, the Germans had not yet become

136

aware of their presence.

'Get down,' Cain ordered when they were about twenty yards on to the bridge. 'Now follow me.'

Panting hard, he squirmed through the ornamental nineteenth-century wrought-ironwork and poised there, bent at the knees. The river lay some twenty feet beneath him. Holding on grimly, his toes dug into the narrow ledge, he waited for them to follow him one by one.

As they joined him, Spiv whispered anxiously. 'What we're gonna do now, Major?'

'You'll see,' Cain hissed.

Seconds passed. Their pursuers had reached the edge of the bridge. Cain could tell by their puzzled shouts to their comrades at the other side that they were completely bewildered by the sudden disappearance of their quarries. But he knew too that bewilderment wouldn't last long. Soon they would begin to search the bridge. The seconds dragged like centuries.

Then he heard what he was waiting for – the steady chug-chug of a barge engine. 'Listen,' he whispered. 'We're directly above the main channel going up to Trier and Metz. Now there's a barge coming. You're all trained parachutists, so when it's directly below us, we drop on it – it's our only chance. They've got us by the short hairs here.'

'And if we miss?' Mac, the non-swimmer,

asked, showing fear for the first time since they had started the operation.

'Then you'd better start learning to swim – quick,' Cain answered. 'All right, come on now – get spread out!'

Tensely they crouched there, hearts beating furiously, nerves jingling. The Germans had begun searching the bridge. They could see their torches flashing. The chug-chug of the barge's engine grew louder. Cain took a deep breath and prepared to jump. The high bow of the tug came into view, the blood-red swastika flag flying proudly in the breeze.

'Not yet,' he warned quickly, as he saw the bridge pass below him, the skipper staring straight ahead, concentrating on the tricky channel. The first barge followed, its tarpaulin-covered deck perhaps some six feet broad, with no sign of any crew on its deck. The second appeared. It was now or never.

'All right,' he bellowed above the noise of the tug's racing motors, *'now!'* A second later he had launched himself into the air, arms flailing as he fought to keep his balance.

SEVEN

The barge skipper was a jaunty young man in his late twenties, his white cap set at a rakish angle on his head of blond curls. And the photographs of naked women, some cut from the weeklies, some personally presented by his conquests, showed that he drove himself as hard on shore as he did on the river.

But now there was nothing jaunty or rakish about him. With the muzzle of Spiv's pistol jammed into his back, he continued to steer the tug, but his face reflected in the mirror was deadly pale and his blue eyes were filled with fear at the sight of these worn, unshaven, haggard men who had appeared from nowhere so suddenly.

'What do you want?' he gasped.

'Shut up!' Spiv rapped, digging his muzzle viciously into the German's back.

'We'll ask the questions,' Abel added, pressing his arm tenderly where he had hurt it during the jump. 'Now, what's your destination?'

'Diedenhofen, I'm taking a cargo of iron ore to one of the steel factories there.'

'He means Thionville in Lorraine,' Abel

139

explained for the benefit of the others, crowded next to him on the narrow bridge, and asked, 'and when do you expect to get there?'

The skipper shrugged slightly. 'Perhaps the day after tomorrow. With the drought we've had the last month, the water line has–'

'What would happen if you didn't make it on time?' Abel interrupted, a plan beginning to form in his mind.

The skipper shrugged again. 'What should happen? The Frogs don't know that this particular barge is coming. But if I'm not back at my home port of Duisburg by the beginning of next week, my chief would want to know why. He would start asking questions.'

'What questions?'

'He'd probably call the steel works at Diedenhofen and check whether I'd left on my way back to Duisburg.'

'So you mean,' Abel said carefully, 'that nobody would be concerned about you if you got lost for – say – eight days?'

The skipper did not answer for a moment. Instead he concentrated on steering the barge train between two red-painted buoys, but the look on his scared face revealed what he was thinking: the sudden intruders had something in mind for him that wouldn't be very pleasant.

Sullenly he answered, 'I suppose not.'

Abel looked at Cain excitedly, 'Did you hear that, Major? Nobody'll miss him for eight days!'

Cain did not react immediately. Since the business at the bridge, he had relaxed into an exhausted lethargy. Even since the lights and the shouting had died away and he had realised they had pulled off the daring escape, he had let Abel take over and capture the tug's skipper. Now he raised his head slowly and asked wearily, 'What do you mean, Abel?'

Eagerly the young American explained. 'We want a place to get our weary heads down, don't we?'

Cain nodded.

'And we want a place where we can get those guys chasing us off our backs?'

Again Cain nodded.

'Well, what's better than where we are now?' Abel announced triumphantly. 'We're making our way to Trier without anyone to stop us and ask awkward questions. The Krauts obviously didn't see us get on the barges, otherwise the *Wasserpolizei* would have been on our tails by now. And this guy here won't be missed for eight days. So what more do we want?'

For a moment the others considered his scheme, while the barges chugged on steadily at five miles an hour. 'You mean,' Spiv said slowly, taking his eyes off the photo of two Eton-cropped middle-aged women without clothes doing something which up to that moment he had thought anatomically impossible, 'we would use this place as a floating base?'

'Sure,' Abel answered eagerly. 'Barges are a dime a dozen on this river. They're everywhere.' He waved a hand at the train of coal barges coming up the other channel. 'So who would care if this guy here anchored his barge somewhere along the bank at Trier? Nobody.'

'But what's to stop him babbling to the nearest rozzer once we were out of sight?' Spiv objected. 'And we'd need him as our cover, don't forget, Yank.'

'Ay,' Mac growled, still angry from the loss of his pack. 'The best way with yon Hun is over the side with him.'

The skipper paled visibly. 'No,' he said urgently in German. 'No, not that. I'll help you. I'm on your side.'

Abel spun round on him. 'On *our* side?' he queried.

'Yes, yes, look.' With fingers that trembled, he set the catch on the big wooden wheel to hold the tug on course, and brushing past Spiv fumbled beneath the pornographic picture of the two Eton-cropped ladies. Something clicked and the picture swung back to reveal a cunningly concealed cavity,

142

containing a bundle of papers. 'For the comrades in France,' he announced, standing back so that they could all see.

'Comrades?' Abel echoed. He reached into the hole and pulled out one of the papers, decorated with the hammer and sickle and headed, *'Aux Camarades des Franc-Tireurs et Partisans.'* Slowly he read the title out aloud and looked at Cain. 'Does it mean anything to you, Major?'

Cain, the veteran of eleven months of clandestine warfare with the Maquis, nodded. 'Yes, the French Communist underground. They have a representative on the *Comité Militaire,* the central Resistance organisation. But it's just a token membership. The Communist partisans go very much their own way. Arrogant bastards for the most part,' he added with sudden venom. 'They maintain they're doing most of the fighting against the Germans. They even have given themselves the heroic title of *Partie des Fusilles* – the party of the shot ones.'

Abel looked at the expectant young skipper. 'Do you mean you're a Communist courier?' he asked.

The skipper jumped at the chance offered him. 'Yes, yes,' he stuttered excitedly. 'That's why I'm on your side. I want to see the Nazis beaten. I'll help you ... *honest.'* Swiftly he explained that most of the river boatmen, travelling permanently between Rotterdam

143

and Basle, Koblenz and Metz, belonged to an international fraternity of Dutch, Swiss, Belgians, Frenchmen and Germans, who had been instinctively anti-authoritarian and, therefore, anti-Nazi right from the start. 'You see,' he said hastily, 'we of the rivers belong together, whatever our nationality and when the Brown ones came along,' he used the German name for the Nazis, 'they wanted to put a stop to all of that. The way they saw it, we were Germans first and rivermen second.'

In thirty-three when the German Communist Party had been forced to go underground, its leaders had immediately contacted their rivermen sympathisers at the great inland port of Duisburg to smuggle out party members most in danger. For years the rivermen had used the International camaraderie of the Rhine and Moselle to spirit Communists from the Reich down to the ports of Antwerp and Rotterdam whence they could be shipped 'to the Workers' Paradise', as the skipper called Russia. Now, since the invasion of the Soviet Russia, the Communist underground in Germany had re-established its links with the great French Communist Party which on Moscow's orders was finally playing a part in the French resistance to the Germans.

'You see,' the young skipper concluded, 'we must show our French comrades that

144

we Germans are not all conquerors – that we, too, are playing a rôle in the fight against Nazi repression.'

Cain sniffed. 'A noble sentiment,' he said unenthusiastically. 'Very noble.'

The young skipper, carried away by his account and already aware by the careless way that Abel now held his pistol that he was out of danger, did not notice the irony. 'So, that's my job when I go into France. I carry the leaflets which detail the fight of the German comrades against the brown-shirted monopoly-capitalists.' He stumbled a little over the big words, but smiled faintly when he had managed to get them out, and waited for the strangers' reaction.

Abel turned to Cain. 'Well?' he demanded.

Cain looked up at him. He could see Abel had already made up his mind. The German skipper was one of the world's good guys, those little people whom he admired so much and who would undoubtedly inherit the earth one day, especially if they were smart enough to vote Communist. For a second he thought of his dealings with the Communists in France and the arrogant leaders of the *Franc-Tireurs et Partisans,* who took their orders from Moscow and whose objectives were not French, but Communist. Yet Abel was right. The Ultra men were beat. They needed a safe place to rest up for a day or so before they set about realising their objective; and what safer place was there than this barge, flying the German flag and unhampered by road blocks, curious civilians or search parties?

'Okay, Abel,' he said finally. 'Your plan is good – I'll buy it. But tell your little friend – one false move and' – he brought down his hook so hard that the point struck deep into the woodwork – 'he won't be long for this earth.'

The German skipper needed no translation. The violent gesture sufficed. He trembled violently.

'*Vanished*,' Kranz exploded, standing there at the edge of fast-flowing, muddy river. 'People don't vanish. *Grosse Kacke am Christbaum!* They just go somewhere.' He took out his cigar stump and pointed to the opposite bank. 'What about your people over there ... didn't they spot anything?'

The young Major with the eye-patch flushed. 'The goulash cannon had just come up and they were having a mug of nigger sweat and a bite to eat. You see they thought that the Tommies were on this side of the river.'

Kranz groaned. 'Heaven, arse and twine, Major! Two Tommies on the run who killed a couple of our cops and probably those headhunters they found dead in the woods on the border late yesterday afternoon, and

146

your men sit down to have breakfast!' Kranz controlled himself with difficulty, but when he spoke again it was in his old measured tone. 'What about the pack ... they found in the farm.' He nodded down the track. 'What do you make of it.'

The Major, happy that the subject of his men's failings had been dropped, responded eagerly, 'The pack itself was made in Belgium. But the plastic explosive it–'

'Plastic explosive?' Kranz queried, sucking at his unlit cigar.

'Yes, it's a new British explosive that can be moulded into handy forms to fit virtually any object that a saboteur might want to blow up. We've got nothing like it. The Tommies drop it a lot to those treacherous hounds of the Resistance.'

Kranz absorbed the information with another of his long silences. On the river, the barges chugged placidly by. Behind him in the village, ox-drawn carts laden with human and animal manure left their odiferous trails behind them as they plodded towards the vineyards. Kranz did not even notice the thick stench.

Obviously the fugitives were skilled operators, trained saboteurs and cold-blooded killers, who had a definite mission within the Reich. And it had to be within the Reich; the expert murder of the head-hunters discovered the day before in the woods demonstrated that the Tommies had definitely intended moving eastwards into Germany.

Kranz frowned angrily, his slanting eyes narrowed to frustrated slits. 'Did you find anything else in the pack?'

'Not much,' the Major said. 'Some stale bread, a small flask that smelled as if it might have once contained whisky, a hunk of Belgian hard cheese,' he yawned wearily, 'and this.' He pulled the dog-eared, thin brown pamphlet from his leather dispatch case. 'That's all, *Her Kommissar.*'

'What is it?'

'A copy of the 1938 prospectus for the Girls' Training College at Trier.'

'*What!*'

The Major with the patch over one eye, smiled tiredly. 'Yes, I thought the same when my sergeant showed it me. What in three devils' name would a bunch of Tommy saboteurs be doing with a pre-war copy of a prospectus for a girls' training college, and in Catholic Trier to boot?' He wrinkled his long nose as another of the stinking ox-carts lumbered by with a rattle of wooden wheels. 'It simply doesn't fit in, does it, Kommissar?'

'No ... it doesn't,' Kranz answered automatically. Yet already in the back of his brain, a couple of odd pieces in the frustrating puzzle were beginning to click into place.

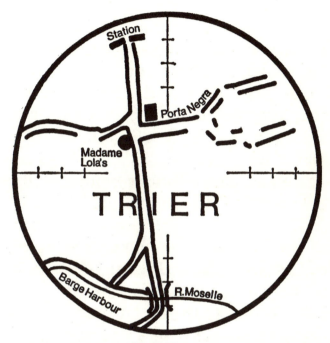

MURDER AT MADAME LOLA'S (August 1942)

ONE

The Moselle was lined, inevitably, with lime and elm trees. But despite the summer heat, the bargees from the great fleet anchored beyond the *Romerbrucke* were not sitting outside under their cool shade. The black-out regulations were too stringent. Instead they were crowded in the little inns which lined the quay where the barge harbour was to be found.

Spiv and Cain walked silently along the quay towards the bridge which had been built by the Romans in the first century when they had first occupied the city, 'old when Rome was young', as the locals boasted. To their right, scores of barges, ranging from tiny Moselle twenty-footers to massive Rhine craft, jammed the harbour in seemingly inextricable confusion. No sound came from them, apart from the faint hush of the hot wind and soft creaking of wood and rope as the wind made them work at their moorings. The barge harbour was asleep.

They walked on to the bridge and strolled casually across it. Freshly washed and shaven, hands in their pockets, they looked like two bargees taking the air, checking the new harbour out, perhaps hoping for some mildly amorous adventure after a hard day on the river. But there was nothing casual about the look in the Ultra men's eyes as they scrutinised the ugly white building perched on the red sandstone cliff from which the Romans had quarried the stone with which to build Trier below.

'Bugger of a place to get into,' Spiv commented out of the corner of his mouth, as they climbed up the narrow path towards it. 'They probably built it up there to stop the local yokels getting the knickers off all them schoolmarms.'

'Probably,' Cain answered softly. Spiv was right. The place was a bugger to get into. With its back to a high sheer outcrop of red rock, it seemed to possess only one entrance, guarded by two wooden-faced sentries, standing rigidly in their red and white striped sentry boxes.

They passed them slowly, taking in the nine-foot-high fence surmounted by spikes, out of the corners of their eyes. In the blue light of the blacked-out lantern above the gate, the sentries watched them suspiciously.

'Move over to the taxi, Spiv,' Cain ordered in a whisper.

Casually they strolled across the road towards the ancient *Opel Wanderer* and its equally ancient driver, his leathery face illuminated by the cigar he was puffing at. On the other side, Spiv made a great play of trying to light a cigarette in the soft wind, while they studied the entrance further. 'Of course, we don't know his nibs is in there, sir,' Spiv said between puffs.

'I agree. But why would they need sentries to guard a bunch of would-be schoolmarms – and members of the Armed SS to boot?'

Spiv laughed softly and finally succeeded in lighting his cigarette. 'They'd need a whole battalion of the buggers if there was really some Judies in there, sir,' he said softly. 'It's been so long since I've had a bit of the other that I've forgotten what it bloody-well looks like. That's for sure!'

Cain laughed too and told himself that nothing seemed to frighten the Cockney wide boy. Whatever the situation, he always had his eye on the main chance – money and women. 'Don't worry, Spiv. Once we're back in London, I'll see you're well looked after on that score.'

'Well looked after!' Spiv snorted. 'I want to be like that squaddie who told his wife when he came home on leave to have a flipping good look at the floor because she wouldn't be seeing anything but the ceiling for the next few days–'

'Shut up!' Cain interrupted urgently. 'There's a staff car coming up. Look!'

At the gate the two SS sentries had

stiffened to the present, their rifles held rigidly to their breasts, their heads turned inwards woodenly as the grey-camouflaged Horch drew up inside the gate.

The sergeant-of-the-guard hurried out of the guard-room, snapped up a tremendous salute and lifted the red and white striped pole. As the two sentries followed the slow progress of the big Horch out of the compound, moving their helmeted heads in unison as if they were worked by wires, Spiv and Cain caught a fleeting glimpse of the enormously fat officer who looked as if he might burst out of his too tight *Luftwaffe* uniform at any minute.

'Meyer – *General der Luftwaffe Meyer!*' Cain breathed, uttering the man's rank in German.

'*Ja, General der Luftwaffe, Meyer,*' a voice next to them echoed. '*Das fette Schwein!*'

The two of them swung round startled, as the Horch started to move smoothly down the hill towards Trier.

It was the ancient taxi driver, who had approached them without their hearing because his feet were enclosed in battered felt slippers. Cain flung Spiv a warning glance. Spiv nodded.

'Do you know him?' Cain asked in his best German.

'Do I know him?' the ancient taxi driver echoed scornfully. 'Oh, yes, I know him all

154

right. Don't I have to bring him back here every night after the fat swine has had it, and not even a tip at three and four o'clock in the morning when anybody who has his senses about him is fast asleep.'

'Had what?' Cain asked puzzled.

'This,' the driver grunted. He held up his bent hand and thrust his thumb between his two forefingers in the Continental symbol for sexual intercourse. 'Every night he's banging up and down on those whores at Lola's, going at it like a fiddler's elbow. The pig! And they've always got to be young uns. If you ask me, if he weren't a shitty general, the police would have him because they're below the legal age.' He spat contemptuously at his slippered feet.

'Where is this – er – Lola's?' Cain asked.

'Lola's?' the driver looked at him curiously. 'I thought every man in Trier knew where Lola's is?'

'We're strangers,' Cain said hastily. 'Off the boats. Up here for the night, that's all.'

'Oh, I see. Well, you see in Catholic Trier, there aren't many whore-houses. The Bishop won't allow it. If the lads over there want a bit,' he indicated the camp, 'they have to go to Luxembourg, they can't afford Lola's prices.'

'But where is Lola's?'

The driver looked at them, obviously assessing them as potential customers. 'You

155

want a jump at Lola's?' he asked, all calculation now. 'She's dear.'

Cain hesitated. Spiv was quicker. He winked knowingly, and made the gesture of counting money with this thumb and forefinger. 'Don't worry, Grandpa,' he said in his strange German, 'we're stacked all right. And ready for a bit too.'

The taxi driver shook his head sorrowfully. 'You foreigners are randy buggers. Well, come on, gentlemen.' He walked over to his ancient Opel and threw open the door ceremoniously, while the two sentries stared at them. 'Madame Lola awaits you.'

The door was opened by a hard-faced aging blond dressed in black knee-high boots laced at the front, her fat body forced into a black satin corset with frills which thrust up her breasts to such an extent that it seemed they would pop out at any moment and fly off of their own volition. 'What do you want?' she asked and stifled a yawn. 'It's Wednesday. We always close early on Wednesdays.'

The taxi driver thrust his head between Cain and Spiv. 'Foreigners,' he said and leered, 'just off the boats. Plenty of money.'

The blonde yawned again, unimpressed. 'All right,' she conceded reluctantly, 'come on in.'

'And what about me?' whined the ancient cab driver.

'Don't worry,' the blonde said, 'you'll get your money at the end of the week as usual from Lola. Bugger off now, will you.'

'All that meat and no potatoes,' Spiv commented under his breath as they followed her hefty, swaying black-clad buttocks down the dark corridor which was heavy with the smell of stale food and ancient lecheries. Somewhere rusty bedsprings were squeaking. Spiv winked at Cain knowingly.

'Here, wait here,' the blonde commanded with a wave of her beringed hand, and gestured at the large room to their right filled with worn, overstuffed red-plush furniture and lit by dim red lights. 'I'll see if I can find Madame.'

When she had swept out, Spiv grinned at Cain's severe look and said: 'Cheer up, sir. It ain't that bad. Tell yerself you're doing it for England.'

Cain muttered an obscenity.

'Can't do that, sir,' Spiv replied smartly. 'I've already got a double-decker bus up there.'

A moment later, Madame Lola herself appeared, fat and blowsy with her black silk-covered bosom thrust out majestically in front of her. She dressed as if she were twenty and looked every day of the sixty she really was. She touched the back of her frizzed, dyed hair and appraised them with calculating eyes.

'Foreigners,' she said at last in a husky voice. 'Have you got money?'

Spiv grinned. 'Money – and something else – in our pants.'

Madame Lola looked down at him as if he were something that had just crawled out of the woodwork. 'I don't like that kind of obscene talk in my establishment,' she said severely.

Spiv feigned amazement. 'What is this place then – the local headquarters of the Salvation Army?'

'Be quiet,' Cain ordered. He didn't like this business one bit, but he knew he had to get upstairs to size up their intended victim and the rooms. Already a vague plan was beginning to form in his mind. 'We're just off the boats down at the Moselle, Madame. Here for the night. We fancied a couple of girls.'

Lola was apparently satisfied with his humility. She looked at the glittering watch which dangled from her impressive bosom. 'We close early on Wednesdays, but I can let you have fifteen minutes. Off you go up the stairs – to your right, you'll find Gerda and Heidi waiting for you.' She raised one blood-tipped, bejewelled finger warningly as they rose to go. 'And remember these are German girls.' She repeated the word 'German', as if it had some special significance. 'So remember, none of your filthy foreign tricks.'

'I'll wrap mine in cellophane paper, if you like, Madame,' Spiv said happily as they went out of the door.

'Okay, off you go to the whores,' Cain ordered when they were alone. 'Give me fifteen minutes. I want to have a quick look round – and no funny business, Spiv.'

Spiv needed no further urgning. He made his way to the end of the corridor to where the whores were waiting in their room like a bee scenting the honey-pot. Hesitantly, Cain made his way along the corridor behind him, pausing at each door and listening there with some embarrassment. But Lola was right. Wednesday was early closing day. Most of the rooms seemed empty. He began to despair of ever finding the General.

But *General der Luftwaffe* Meyer was still there. Suddenly ahead of Cain in the long, dimly lit corridor a door was flung open. The Major straightened up. A naked girl, clutching an empty champagne bottle in her tiny hand, staggered out and reeled towards him. As she came level with him, she giggled, 'Champus … the General wants more champus.' She swayed on towards the stairs. Cain breathed out. She did not look a day over fourteen. But there was nothing girlishly innocent about her.

Cautiously Cain moved to the open door. Opposite it there was a long wall mirror in which he could see what was happening in the room without being seen himself. Carefully he pressed himself against the wall in the shadows and peered into the mirror. Meyer, his enormously fat stomach hanging in a bulging curve over his flaccid organ, was completely naked, save for his boots. One pudgy hand was closed over the budding breast of an equally naked teenage girl, whose long blonde hair hung in wild disarray over her flushed, drunken face, while his other hand was pressed up between her smooth young legs so forcefully that the girl struggled wildly like an animal caught in a trap.

Cain was sickened. He knew the girl was a whore and a willing victim – after all she was getting paid for it – nevertheless he was repelled by the vile corruption of the scene.

Suddenly Meyer turned his attention from the girl and looked at the door. For an instant, Cain caught a glimpse of the Grey Wolf's face. Set in a mass of fat, his piglike eyes were those of the sensualist: a man whose life was centred exclusively on the pleasures of the flesh. He opened his thick-lipped, wet mouth and shouted in a barrack-room voice coarsened by years of heavy drinking in the mess and shouting commands at bewildered recruits, 'Where in three devils' name is that champus, girlie?'

'Coming, *Herr General*,' the other teenage

whore called from the bottom of the stairs.

'Well, get your arse up here with it at once, you silly cow!' he roared back, and slid his big white hand between the blonde's legs again. She giggled and let herself be touched.

As Cain ducked away down the corridor before the girl with the champagne discovered him there, he told himself grimly that it would be easy to kill the gross general. Indeed it would give him a good deal of pleasure to put an end to his corrupt existence.

TWO

'All right, Horst,' Cain said to the tugboat skipper, 'you can go now. We won't need you any more, but keep an eye out there on deck, please.'

Obediently the blond German left them crouched around the large crate which served as a table in the hideout they had constructed for themselves in the hold of the middle barge. Cain waited until he had climbed the ladder, thrown back the tarpaulin and disappeared. Despite the fact that Horst was an anti-Nazi and anyway didn't understand English, Cain did not altogether trust him. He preferred that the handsome young German should not know more about their activities than was absolutely necessary.

Now, with a stub of lead pencil, he drew a cross on the top of the crate. 'The Porta Negra,' he explained, 'an old Roman gate right in the centre of Trier – here... The main street runs by it along here up to the railway station – here.' He made another rough cross on the wood. 'Here is where Madame Lola has what we used to call delicately in my youth a house of ill-repute.'

'For them of you who isn't educated like me and the Major,' Spiv added, 'that means a knocking shop.'

'As I see it,' Cain continued, 'that place on the hill is too tough a nut for us to crack with what we have at our disposal. Surrounded by high fence with only one entrance guarded by sentries, it's out of the question.' He held up his hook as if to ward the Scot off physically, 'And it's no use looking at me like that, Mac. We can't blast our way in. Besides we've got no P.E. now either. So I've made my mind up. It's got to be the brothel here.' He tapped the table with his hook. 'We kill the Grey Wolf there.'

'What a way to go,' Spiv breathed reverently. 'At least, he'll die happy.'

'Now, I realise there are plenty of difficulties about carrying out an op of that kind in the middle of a city. For a start there'll be witnesses. But the main thing is that we can get into the place easily. As long as you've got money, there's always an open door at Madame Lola's.'

'So how are we going to do it?' Mac asked.

'First the time,' Cain replied. 'As far as we could gather last night, the Grey Wolf usually sends his staff car away after he has arrived at Lola's and then calls a taxi when he's ready to leave to take him back to his HQ. Now according to our informant, that is normally in the early hours of the morning. Which is to our advantage of course. If we can pull it off then, the centre of town should be pretty dead. So if we were positioned near Madame Lola's perhaps here,' he marked the crate, 'with one of us inside—'

'I volunteer,' Spiv said, quickly raising his hand.

'Shut up!' shouted the other three in unison.

'—and move in on the fat swine at the moment the taxi makes its appearance, we should be able to catch him at the door and make our escape before anybody is really aware of what is happening.'

'Yes, what about the escape?' Abel asked a little anxiously. 'I've been meaning to ask you about that.'

'As I've planned it, the simplest way out of Trier once the balloon goes up, is by this barge. Horst will have orders to up anchor as soon as we get back on board.'

'And our destination?' Abel queried.

'With a bit of luck we could get as far as Metz. From there it shouldn't be too difficult to link up with one of the Maquis sections in the Champagne area. They could arrange by radio with London to get the 138th Squadron to come and pick us up. And even if we don't make it to Metz, Luxembourg and France are just up the river and there we'll be relatively safe. The main thing, I think, is to get out of Trier before they clamp down on all exits from the city. And this barge is the ideal way of doing that.'

Abel nodded. But Spiv wasn't so sure. 'But it's a good mile from that knocking shop of Lola's back to the barge, Major,' he objected. 'What if it's payday in the German Army and the knocking shops around there are full of Jerry squaddies? Tired and happy they might be after a bit, but if they see their general shot down in front of them, they're bound to react.'

'I know what you mean, Spiv, but I've thought of that eventuality too. That's where Mac comes in.' He turned to the Scot. 'Mac, do you think that you could do this for me?' Swiftly he explained his scheme for which he would need Mac's cunning inventive fingers, and by the time he had finished, he could see by the looks on the others' faces that he had finally convinced them that his rough and ready plan had a chance of succeeding.

He let them absorb the details for a few moments, raise any objections they might have had, then said. 'You'll probably want to know when we're going to carry out the op, eh?'

Again they nodded.

'So it's my suggestion that we do a dummy run tonight, check out the difficulties, etc, and then if the Grey Wolf decides to indulge himself in one of his little orgies tomorrow night,' his jaw hardened, 'it'll be his last!'

By the time Cain had started actively planning the Grey Wolf's assassination outside the brothel, *Oberkommissar* Kranz had commenced putting the story of the missing Englishmen into some sort of shape. From the Eupen office of the Gestapo he learned that the fat woman found dead in the ditch with the brutally murdered Field Gendarmes was well known there on account of her anti-German sentiments. Obviously, he concluded, she had been recruited by the Tommies to guide them deeper into Germany. So the whole business wasn't just a chance affair, it had been planned right from the start. The Tommies had a definite objective within Germany and it had something to do with Trier.

For several hours while he was waiting for

further news of the extensive search being carried out along both banks of the Moselle where the Tommies had last been seen, he had pored over the pre-war Guide, examining the maps of Trier it contained to check whether any particular location had been marked. Without success. He had worked his way through the list of lecturers to see whether any of their names had been checked off. Again he drew a blank. For a while, after the one-eyed Major in charge of the search reported that no trace of the Englishmen had been found, he dropped the idea that the guide had anything to do with an objective in Trier. Perhaps it was being used as a key to some code or other in conjunction with a one-time pad? But a phone call to the Cologne branch of the *Abwehr* soon disillusioned him. The smooth-talking *Abwehr* agent on the other end of the line felt it was 'hardly likely' that a British operator would use a text written in German for the key to his code. Besides a guide like that would not have sufficient range of vocabulary to be suitable as a key. So that avenue was blocked too. He returned to his original idea that the fugitives' objective was something to do with Trier itself.

And then it came to him. *The Training College itself was the objective.*

For a while he sat on the idea. What the hell would the killers be after in a girls' training college? He didn't want to make himself look foolish by making inquiries in that direction; the *Oberkommissar* Kranz was very proud of his reputation as the 'Sly One'. But in the end when he could see no other possibility, he decided to take a chance even if it did mean that he might be laughed at. He called the Training College.

To his surprise, a gruff male voice answered with a militarily precise: 'Special Supply Unit Number 55. Bocholt. At your command!'

'Isn't this the girls' Training College?'

Bocholt laughed. 'Sometimes I think it is – the things that go on here! No, it's not.'

'Listen,' Kranz said, sensing the first feeling of hope. 'My name's Kranz – Senior Commissar Kranz – of the Secret State Police.'

Kranz could almost feel the other man's fear at the mention of the dreaded Gestapo. It was an old reaction and he had experienced it many a time, but still it gave him a thrill of power.

'Yes, Commissar, how can I help you?' Bocholt's voice was suddenly very formal and afraid.

'Tell me what kind of outfit are you up there in Trier?'

'We're supposed to be a supply outfit, Commissar,' Bocholt replied. 'Though what we supply to whom, I wouldn't know. And I don't know why we've got to have SS sentries on the gate either. But then I'm only a clerk typist and generals don't often take clerks into their confidence, do they, Commissar?'

Kranz could imagine Bocholt: a weedy unctuous little runt probably with Wehrmacht glasses. 'Yes,' he agreed, 'but who is this general of yours?'

'*General der Luftwaffe* Meyer, Commissar.'

'An Air Force general running an Army supply outfit,' Kranz exclaimed, 'that seems a bit strange.'

'Everything's strange here, Commissar.'

Suddenly Kranz realised he was on to something. The Number 55 Special Supply Unit obviously wasn't what it was supposed to be. 'Thank you, Bocholt, you've been a great help,' he said.

The unknown clerk at the other end gave a faint sigh of relief. 'At any time, Senior Commissar,' he breathed, glad that this conversation with a member of the feared Gestapo was over and he was still not in trouble.

'Shitty liar!' Kranz told himself and put the phone down. For a few moments he sat there, a thoughtful look in his slanting sadist's eyes. Then he rose to his feet, his mind made up.

He opened the window of the inn and called out to the young one-eyed Major, who was staring gloomily into space, his

168

jackboots grey with mud from the abortive search along the Moselle. 'Major!'

He swung round. 'Yes?'

'Can you arrange to have the car sent round at once – and by the way, you'd better get those boots of yours polished.'

The Major looked up at him as if he had suddenly gone off his head. 'Get my boots polished?' he echoed. 'Why?'

Kranz laughed softly at his bewilderment, unlit cigar stump still stuck to his thick bottom lip. 'Because, *mein lieber Herr Major,* we're going to visit a general.'

THREE

'*Heil Hitler!*'

General der Luftwaffe Meyer, wedged behind the desk, his enormous belly bulging over its top, looked up slowly and raised his pudgy, bedimpled hand casually. '*Heil Hitler,*' he echoed and appraised Kranz standing rigidly to attention in front of him, his hands pressed to the sides of his long leather coat, as if he were a young recruit. 'All right, Commissar,' he said in his drink-thickened voice, 'you can stand at ease. You're not in the Service, you know.'

Kranz relaxed a little. 'We of the Gestapo,

169

sir, regard ourselves as members of the Forces. We feel we are doing our little bit to help them to achieve final victory.'

Mayer looked at him contemptuously with his red, piglike eyes. 'I have never liked policemen, Commissar, whether they were military or civilian, and I especially dislike you super policemen of the Gestapo.'

Kranz kept control of himself. If the fat, bemedalled General weren't afraid of him, it meant he had to have powerful protectors in the Party. Therefore the insulting contemptuous fat swine would have to be treated carefully; he didn't want to find himself posted to some God-forsaken Gestapo outpost in the Ukraine, cross-examining a lot of lice-ridden, dumb Russian partisans.

'May I sit down, General?'

'I suppose so. But remember I'm a very busy man. And you'd better have a good excuse for bursting in on me like this and nearly giving those pansy adjutants of mine a heart attack. I have powerful friends at court, Commissar.' Again he treated Kranz to a contemptuous look and the Gestapo man realised that his original impression had been right: the General had the face of a man who had been everywhere, seen and done everything: a man who wouldn't be easily impressed. And Meyer was a man of influence.

'I am sorry about that, General. But as I

hope to explain, there was a very good reason for my sudden appearance here.' He licked suddenly dry lips. 'Would the General object to telling me the nature of his post here in Trier?' he asked, using the old-fashioned indirect form of speech.

'I would,' Meyer snapped. 'It is top-secret – on the Führer's express orders.'

'I see.' Again Kranz hesitated. 'Then may I be permitted to put it like this, sir? Would your job here be important enough for the Tommies to send in trained killers to ... er, to assassinate you, General?'

Meyer looked at him sharply, but there was no trace of fear in his bloodshot little eyes. 'What did you say – assassinate me?'

Swiftly Kranz explained what he knew and what he had guessed, while Meyer listened, his gross face motionless. 'So you see, General,' he concluded, 'I have good reason to think that those men have been sent specially by London to kill you.'

Meyer stared at him, as if he were seeing the Gestapo man for the first time. 'I can't tell you my mission,' he said carefully. 'But I can tell you this. Under certain circumstances, it could be of vital importance to the Reich. Perhaps if I were – assassinated, as you say – it would be difficult to replace me with another general officer from the Führer Reserve – I have certain specialist qualifications, you see.' He shrugged and his fat jowls trembled. 'I suppose it might be worth those Tommies' while to get rid of me, if they ever became aware of my possible mission. Though I can assure you, Commissar,' he added hastily, 'our security here is first class. Only a handful of us know what the mission is.'

'Of course, of course, sir,' Kranz said, eager to please. 'I can see that. An old policeman like me always spots sloppy security right off. But somehow or other, the Tommies have got on to you, and they're going to try to kill you.'

'All right, I'll accept your word for it. But you say yourself they have disappeared. Perhaps they drowned in the Moselle?'

Kranz shook his head firmly, confident now that he had gained the General's support. 'I don't think so, sir... They'd be trained men... Somehow or other they slipped through those dummies of the reserve regiment I used to search for them and got clean away... But they'll turn up again... Take my word for that, sir.'

'I see – and what do you intend to do about it?'

'Well, sir, I'd ... like to lure them out of their hiding place.' He hesitated. 'I don't know quite how to put this?'

'Then let me do it for you, Commissar,' Meyer snapped. 'For the last thirty years or so, people have been trying to kill me in one way or the other – in France in the old war, in China, later in Spain. So far they haven't succeeded, as you can see – and,' he chuckled grimly, 'I make a big enough target, don't I? So what do you want me to do to lure these people out of their holes – present a moving target, eh?'

Slowly Kranz nodded his head. 'Yessir, this is what I would like you to do.'

As the hot summer day wore on, Kranz, still clad in his long leather coat and sweating heavily as a result, convinced now that Meyer was the Englishmen's target, set his plan in motion. He knew he must not frighten them off by making his precautions too obvious. They must be lured into making the attack, if they were really hiding in Trier. Too many guards around the General would certainly make them change their minds. Hence he replaced the General's bespectacled elderly driver with an SS man, who had won the Iron Cross for bravery in Russia. Two other SS men, with machine-pistols hidden beneath their desks, were established among the clerks in the General's outer office. The General's two elegant adjutants – whom he referred to contemptuously, as 'homosexual wet dreams' – were forced to sacrifice their immaculate officer uniforms to another couple of SS privates, and the big pistols they carried at their belts were no longer there solely for decorative purposes; they were fully loaded, safety catches off, ready to be used at the first sign of trouble.

The General cooperated fully in the new security measures. He, too, had suddenly developed a great interest in having the would-be killers caught. 'Not because I'm afraid, Kranz,' he had snapped. 'But for Germany's sake. If I'm killed, it could have very serious consequences.' All the same, Meyer had insisted that he must follow his normal daily routine. 'My mission demands that I continue my work, Kranz,' he'd explained, 'even if my life is in danger. There is so damn much to be done, and I'm the only one who can do it. You see, in two days' time I'm moving my HQ to Metz in Lorraine. My work here in Trier will be finished then and I shall be carrying out the next stage of my mission from there. By that time, I want all this routine shit out of the way.' He sighed, his gross face softening for the first time since Kranz had met him, 'I can hardly find time to indulge myself in modest pleasures I've so much to do.' His piglike eyes sparkled and Kranz wondered what kind of 'modest pleasures' the General was referring to.

But as the red ball of the sun started to sink below the hills beyond the sparkling silver of the Moselle in the valley below, Kranz was too occupied with his security precautions to deliberate very long on the subject.

It was after dinner at the little Officers' Casino in the hilltop HQ that Meyer sighed expansively, rubbing his hands across his great girth with satisfaction, and said, 'Well, Kranz you know the old German saying, *nach dem Essen soll man rauchen und eine Frau gebrauchen?*'

Kranz nodded warily. The General, who had eaten three plates of the rich chicken fricassée in cream sauce belched and reached in his pocket for his cigar case. He tendered it to the Gestapo man, whose face was flushed from the heavy wine which the General had insisted he drink with his meal.

'Goering himself gave me these cigars,' Meyer said. 'So they must be good. So first we smoke and then we indulge ourselves in a little bit of female company.'

'How do you mean, *Herr General?*'

'Well, my dear policeman,' Meyer said happily. 'When you get to my great age, you need some pretty powerful medicine to activate the old Peterman, and it just happens that in Trier there is a certain establishment which provides the right kind of medicine for me. You understand I have specific special tastes.'

Kranz did not understand. His own wife was plump, plain and forty and wore flannel bloomers most of the time, but she still provided the kind of sex which aroused him. 'Do you mean that we are going to leave this place tonight, *Herr General?*'

'I do,' Meyer belched again.

'But the danger–'

Meyer waved him to silence. 'The only danger that can possibly face me at Madame Lola's, my dear policeman, is that I can't afford the simple pleasures I allow myself there – or perhaps that my poor ageing Peterman does not respond to the ministrations of those little darlings whom you will meet.' *General der Luftwaffe* Meyer pushed back his chair with an air of finality. All around the other officers rose to their feet hastily. Meyer waved them to their seats again. 'Now Kranz,' he said, as his orderly raced for his hat and belt, 'don't look so worried. Whoever heard of anyone being assassinated in a house of joy, eh?'

FOUR

The cobbled streets of the city were virtually empty. The heat of the day had gone. The wind had increased in strength, coming down from the hills all around Trier and bringing with it cold air. There was the smell

176

of rain in the blacked-out ancient streets.

Cain, a bottle of beer clutched as camouflage in his good hand, looked up at he sky. Tattered dark clouds scudded by overhead, occasionally parting to reveal the silver half moon. He grunted with satisfaction. It was an ideal night for their mission. Not too dark, but dark enough; and the sudden cold snap was keeping the occasional passer-by from lingering too long in the silent streets on his way home.

'Okay, Spiv, let's go over,' he said softly.

Moving together almost noiselessly in their rubber-soled shoes, they crossed to the dark squat silhouette of the Porta Negra the Roman ruin, from which they could safely observe the comings and goings at Madame Lola's opposite. Abel strolled casually towards Lola's, a rolled-up local paper bought at the all-night stall at the main station, in his hand. Somewhere in the gloom beyond, Mac would be setting his trap.

Somewhere a church clock chimed ten. Now the cold streets were completely empty. Even the elderly policemen who patrolled the centre of the city seemed to have sought refuge from the sudden cold inside the warm inns. The only sound was the occasional creak of Lola's door opening to admit or release customers. 'Bugger it,' Spiv grumbled. 'I think the old boy is probably in his kipp by now, snoring his fat head off.'

'Maybe,' Cain answered non-committally. He glanced at the glowing dial. 'But there's still time. He might come yet.'

It was just as the first drops of rain had begun to fall, splattering noisily on the cobbles, that they heard the sound of a powerful motor crawling slowly through the twisting, blacked-out streets. They were alert at once, the cold, the rain, their boredom forgotten now. Two faint blue headlights were moving slowly towards their position from the direction of the river.

Across the road, Abel had heard the sound too. He thrust his paper, now limp with the rain, into his pocket and started to saunter towards Lola's. Cain couldn't see Mac. But he knew he was crouching there somewhere in the shadows to their rear, ready to cover their escape when the time came.

The car came closer. Overhead the moon suddenly broke from the tattered clouds and momentarily cast its pale light on to the wet-gleaming street. It was long enough for them to see that the car moving towards Lola's establishment was the General's big Horch.

'It's him, Spiv,' Cain whispered urgently. 'Stand by.'

'Do we do him now?'

'No, we stick to the plan. Let him get inside and rid of the staff car. Then when the taxi comes to fetch him after his bit of fun, we let him have it.'

Spiv opened his mouth to protest, but Cain snapped at him to be quiet, as the Horch's brakes, squeaking as if they were wet, pulled the car to a halt outside the brothel.

But unlike the previous evening when they had done their dummy run, the staff car did not draw away after the general had got out. Instead the driver turned off his motor, as if he were preparing to stay there; and in the shaft of yellow light which flashed from the brothel door, they could see now that another man had remained seated in the back of the car. Cain drew in his breath sharply.

At his side, Spiv hissed, 'Are you thinking what I'm thinking, sir?'

As the door closed again the heavily-set big man disappeared into the darkness of the car once more, Cain nodded tensely. 'Yes. That chap's got Gestapo written all over him.'

'Right in one, sir. My thinking entirely – a rozzer. I can smell 'em a mile off. What–'

Cain pressed his arm suddenly. The question died on the little Cockney's lips.

'Look!' Cain ordered. 'Up the street.'

About fifty yards away two big men were strolling slowly but purposefully down the street. They were too far away for Cain to make out the details. But he could make out one thing – their right arms seemed longer

179

than their left. They were carrying pistols.

'More of them,' he said urgently.

'And there's two more of the buggers over there – down the street, sir.'

Cain swung round. A couple more of the silent, purposeful figures had detached themselves from the shadows, and were coming in their direction.

'They've rumbled!' Spiv put Cain's thoughts into words. 'They're on to us, sir.'

'Yes,' Cain snapped. 'I don't know whether they've tumbled to the fact that we're here at this very moment. But they've obviously slapped a special guard on the Grey Wolf.'

'Is the op off?'

'Yes, and we'd better get the hell out of here smartish–' He stopped short. Abel had spotted the approaching men with the pistols in their hands and ducked into the nearest shop doorway. But he was still carrying the damned paper and it seemed to an anxious Cain that it stuck out like a signpost advertising the American's presence. It would be only a matter of seconds and they'd see him.

'Listen, Spiv,' he said. 'They're going to tumble to Captain Abel in a minute. We've got to draw attention to ourselves and give him a chance to make a break for it.'

'What about the other buggers? They're blocking the way to the barge.'

'I know. But we've got to try. And we've

got the element of surprise on our side. By the time they start thinking of challenging, we'll have 'em.'

'All right, sir, I'm game,' Spiv answered swiftly, but his voice wasn't too steady. 'Bash on, sir.'

'Right then now!'

They broke from their cover and started walking quietly but swiftly towards the two shadows who barred their way. Behind them the other two had stopped, alerted by the sudden footsteps. Abel was still hidden from him. Cain prayed that once the trouble started, he would have the good sense to start running like the devil.

For a fleeting moment the pale moon slipped out from a rain cloud and flung a thin shaft of light on the two men standing there, their silhouettes suddenly alert and tense. 'They've spotted us,' Cain whispered. 'But keep going fast.' The moon vanished again and left the street in darkness once more.

They were almost on to the men now. 'Don't use your pistol if you can help it, Spiv,' Cain ordered. 'All right, the balloon's about to go up.'

'Halt!' a thick voice, used to giving commands and having them obeyed, broke the night silence.

'Keep moving,' Cain hissed.

The man who had spoken hesitated. They

were only a matter of feet away from him and his companion now. They could see clearly that both the Germans were holding pistols in their right hands.

'*Halt! Stehenbleiben, sage ich!*' commanded the voice once more.

Cain breathed in. This was it. Their challenger would wait a couple of seconds more before he took action, and those couple of seconds were all he and Spiv needed. '*Now!*' he ordered, exhaling with a fierce energy.

They broke into a run. '*Was?*' the bigger of the two Germans began. His words ended with a scream of agony as Cain slashed the fearsome hook across his surprised face. Next to Cain, Spiv jammed his knee into the other German's crotch. As he doubled up, choking with vomit, Spiv rammed up his kneecap once more – right under his jaw, breaking his neck instantly.

Behind them there was a hoarse shout of rage. Cain swung round. 'Abel, run for it!' he yelled desperately.

The American broke from his cover and started pelting down the pavement, head hunched between his shoulders like a football player.

'*Stehenbleiben oder ich schiesse!*' someone cried.

Abel kept running.

Scarlet flame stabbed the night as a pistol cracked. A slug struck the pavement just behind Abel, sending up a flurry of blue sparks, and whined off into the night. Abel pelted on.

'Over here,' Cain gasped. 'Quick!'

Next to him, Spiv crouched, and steadying his sawn-off .38 with both hands, fired. One of the men beginning to run after Abel screamed. He skidded to a sudden halt and fell heavily to the wet cobbles. The next moment Abel had reached them, his chest heaving violently. But Cain knew they had no time to waste. The driver of the Horch was starting its motor. They would be after them in it in a moment!

'Come on, let's hook it!' he cried.

They began running together, but well spaced out. Behind them pistols cracked again. Cain felt a burning pain in his bad arm. 'Shit,' he cursed, 'I've been hit!' But he continued running.

Mac loomed out of the darkness. 'Get your gear ready, Mac,' Cain cried through gritted teeth. 'They're after us in a car.'

'Ay, a right ballsup!' Mac grunted, dragging the chain he had fashioned in the barge across the road, the spikes of the crows' feet pointing upwards. Swiftly he dropped it into place and began running after them.

Now the Horch had turned. In first gear it was racing noisily down the blacked-out street. In Lola's the windows had been flung open. Angry, frightened voices were shouting questions and orders. Somewhere a policeman was blowing his whistle frantically to summon aid. Spiv paused and fired a wild shot behind him at the Horch. It missed. He cursed and ran on after the others.

The front tyre of the Horch ran into the crows' feet. The tyre burst with a bang like a shell exploding, bringing the Horch to a violent halt. The driver slumped with his head through the suddenly shattered windscreen, the car's motor running idly. But Cain, his sleeve full of blood now, knew that the pursuit had only let up for a moment. Already the door of the Horch had been flung open. The man who had sat in the back was shouting orders in a violent, angry voice.

'Down that alley,' he panted. 'We'll try to shake them off.'

They changed direction swiftly. A high wall loomed up in front of them.

'Up the wall!' gasped Cain.

Mac sprang upwards and caught the jagged top. He hauled himself up. Spiv followed. Behind them the noise of the pursuit was getting louder agin. Abel grabbed for the top. He missed his hold and screamed with pain as the jagged surface ripped his nails.

'For Christ's sake, shut up!' Cain hissed angrily.

Spiv and Mac leaned down and grabbed Abel's hands. They tugged and he was up.

An instant later Cain had followed him. They dropped into the grass on the other side. In the darkness Mac blundered into a glass cloche. It splintered under his boots. He crunched over it, cursing vociferously. They came to a gate. Panting wildly Spiv flung it open and ducked back instantly.

'What is it?' Cain demanded.

'A lorry with a searchlight,' he gasped. 'Look out!'

The light blinked on. They dropped to the wet grass. Slowly the searchlight began to probe each shadow, each doorway, running from side to side of the darkened street, moving on when satisfied.

'All right,' Cain said, 'Mac, you're our best shot. Knock it out. Then the lot of you – over the road and run like hell down that alley-way over there. Clear?'

'Clear!' they whispered in unison.

'Okay, Mac. *Now!*'

Standing upright, Mac took careful aim as the icy light came closer. There was the sudden noise of breaking glass as the light went out abruptly, blinding them and their pursuers.

'Let's go!' Cain yelled and rose.

An instant later they were running crazily for the alley opposite, tracer stitching the air in angry, wild confusion.

FIVE

The chase caught up with them again just as they reached the barge harbour. They had just sprung aboard their own barge, its engine already throbbing regularly, when the first of their pursuers came into view.

He was not running, but walking stealthily, pistol in hand, peering into the wheelhouses and deck cabins of the barges. A couple of yards behind him another German detached himself from the shadows and began to do the same thing.

Cain, his face pale and grey with the pain of his arm, hissed at the Skipper, 'Horst, take her away. Nice and quiet, if you can. Make it appear you're making a routine departure.'

'Don't worry,' Horst answered, his voice shaky but determined. 'The Gestapo bastards won't get us!'

Cain threw him a glance. In the faint blue light of the wheelhouse his face was an unnatural ashen colour and he was obviously very afraid, but he wasn't going to let them down.

More and more Germans were coming down to the quay from the direction of the city. Further off, he could hear the sound of a motor grinding along in first gear, as if its occupants were searching for something in the darkness. He could guess what. Slowly Horst started to manoeuvre the tug and its barges towards the main channel. It could be only a matter of moments before they were challenged.

'Stand by,' Cain ordered. 'Once the bastards start asking questions, don't hesitate – shoot to kill. We've got to get out of here. Okay, I'll take the bridge. Spiv, double up to the bows! Mac and Abel – over to the side!'

'Ay, ay, captain,' rapped Spiv.

Swiftly they took up their positions and waited, half crouched in the darkness, while to their left the enemy continued to search the barges lining the quay, as if they were as yet unaware that their quarry was escaping them.

Suddenly the car that had been grinding along in first gear swung into view. A rough voice shouted something. A torch clicked on and a white beam of light swung along the quay. Cain tensed.

The tug began to pick up speed. The dark shape of the *Roemerbrucke,* supposedly built by the Romans themselves eighteen centuries before, loomed up. Above the chug-chug of the tug's engines, Cain could hear the clatter of heavy army boots running across it. He raised his pistol.

Down below they were still in the shadows, but the man on the bridge was brutally exposed as he leaned over and shouted something into the darkness. Steadying his hand on the ledge Cain took careful aim. The pistol jumped in his hand. The man on the bridge fanned the air with his hands. His weapon clattered to the cobbles as he tumbled over the edge of the bridge and fell into the Moselle. Someone yelled a warning. A slug nicked a hoist with a hollow clang and whined off into the darkness as they started to slide under the cover of the ancient bridge.

'Keep her going, Horst!' Cain cried enthusiastically, 'you're doing fine.' Forgetting the pain in his wounded arm in his excitement, he doubled out of the bridge and took up his position next to the big smoking funnel, waiting for the moment when the tug would emerge on the other side. Behind them lead was striking the wooden barges with dull, solid thuds.

They started to slide out into the open. Two men were waiting for them on the other side of the bridge: stark angry silhouettes against the faint silver light of the sky. A machine-pistol chattered. Angry red fire stitched a pattern along the deck at his feet. Slugs beat the thin metal of the funnel in a hollow tattoo. Cain swung up his pistol. But Mac and Spiv were quicker. They fired in unison.

One of the Germans screamed with pain. His companion was luckier. Mac's bullet missed him, striking the stone balustrade in a flurry of red sparks. He responded with a burst of angry machine-pistol fire which struck the bridge. The glass in front of Horst shattered into a crazy spider's web, temporarily blinding him. Desperately he raised one hand from the wheel and smashed his big fist through the shattered glass.

But the damage had been done. As the barge train nosed its way deeper into the main channel, the second man on the bridge flung himself flat on to the cobbles and yelled a warning to the men on the quay. An excited crackle of smallarms fire erupted the length of the bank.

Cain bit his lip angrily. He had never appreciated that a barge moved so bloody slowly. They couldn't be moving more than 10 mph. 'Horst, can't you get her going more quickly?' he rapped.

The German skipper, with blood dripping unheeded from his mangled hand to the red puddle at his feet, shook his head grimly, eyes concentrated on his front. 'It's the shitty barges,' he gasped, 'they're holding us back! If we could cut—'

'Leave it to me,' Cain interrupted.

He slipped outside, body bent double, as the snap-crackle of smallarms fire intensified. 'Keep it up,' he yelled to the others, sprawled behind the cover of the tug's sides, returning the fire the best they could. 'I'm going to get rid of the barges!'

Suddenly the moon slipped from behind the clouds, clearly illuminating the escaping barge. 'There's one of them!' a coarse voice shouted on the quay. 'Don't let the shitty bastard escape!'

Bullets pattered against the metal like heavy summer rain. Cain desperately fought his way forward. Behind him, Mac and the others did their best to cover him, popping up from beneath their cover, getting off a quick shot and ducking again at lightning speed. Grimly the one-armed Major edged his way forward, inch by inch. The bow rope seemed a million miles away at that moment. A slug hit his hook, sending fierce pain up his wounded arm, but he kept on doggedly. And then, with the bullets striking the stern all around him, the sweat dripping from his strained face in opaque pearls, he slashed his hook at the rope. Once ... twice ... three times. Like a snake, it curled off into the darkness and all of a sudden the tug was churning forward, relieved of the tremendous load. Cain let his sweat-soaked face slump to the wet deck in exhaustion.

'*Scheisstommies!*' Kranz cursed, rising to his feet. In the gutter the young SS man, who had shouted the warning that the Tommies were escaping, lay choking in his own blood, shot through the throat by Spiv.

He clapped his hands around his mouth and bellowed, 'Bring that shitty car up here, driver!... You,' he spun round at one of the SS men dressed in the borrowed adjutant's uniform, 'on your hind legs and get to the phone. Tell General Meyer what has happened here. At the double, man!'

The commandeered police car squealed to a halt next to the dying man gurgling incoherently in the gutter. A middle-aged policeman edged himself out.

'Move your fat green arse,' Kranz cried angrily, enraged by his ponderous official slowness, 'see what you can do for that poor lad down on the ground there.'

He pushed past the cop and flopped into his seat in the car. 'Driver, where's the River Police HQ?'

'About two kilometres from here, Commissar. At the far side of the city.'

'Switch on your shitty siren then,' Kranz snapped, angry, 'and let's get there. Those Tommy shitehawks are not going to get away if preventing them is the last thing I do!'

The police launch appeared as if from nowhere. Horst flung the wheel to one side. The tug heeled just as scarlet flame spat from the launch's twin heavy machine-guns.

Tracer – red, white and green – zipped viciously through the darkness just behind them. A voice boomed through the loudhailer: 'Stop your engines, barge!... At once! Otherwise we'll be forced to blast you–'

The words ended in a scream as Mac fired a wild shot at extreme range. The twin machine-guns opened up again at once. Bullets ripped the length of the tug.

'Hold tight!' Horst screamed.

Only able to use one hand now, he swung the wheel round. The police launch shot by in a furious flurry of white water, missing their bow by inches. The police launch swung in again in a streaming circle, its machine-guns chattering furiously. They ducked as the slugs sawed through the top of the funnel. It hung there grotesquely for an instant, then dropped into the boiling water. Slowly but inevitably the tug started to lose speed.

Standing groggily at the wheel, his face now smeared with blood, Horst yelled, 'Get into the water while you can... I can hold 'em for a little while longer... That's Wasserbillig over there ... Luxembourg...'

'But you're coming with us!' Abel yelled back, thrusting his pistol in his belt ready to dive overboard, as the launch came in for another attack.

Horst laughed wearily and winced with pain, 'I can't swim... Damned funny, isn't it?'

'I can't let you–' Abel began, but Cain grabbed his arm viciously, as the engines of the launch screamed with fury only fifty feet or so away, 'come on – over the side, while we've still got a chance!'

Abel caught one last glimpse of the wounded German's face. It was sweat-stained, covered with blood from glass splinters, and terribly afraid. Yet it was the face of a man who went to his death willingly. Then as the machine-guns rattled into noisy action once more, he dropped over the side into the dark river. A moment later he was striking out powerfully after the rest towards the faint smudge of the Luxembourg shore.

SIX

Horst sat slumped on a stool exactly in the centre of the evil-smelling police interrogation room, enclosed in the circle of hard white light from the single, wire-enclosed bulb above him in the ceiling. Slowly Kranz thrust his angry-red unshaven face into Horst's.

'Red bastard!' he hissed. 'We know all about you. Do you know that? When I've finished with you, traitor, you'll be happy to allow the executioner to chop off your turnip.

In fact, you'll plead with him to do so.'

Horst said nothing. He kept his eyes fixed on the dirty, tiled floor, the blood slowly drying on his face from the beating. The locals had worked him over for nearly an hour. His nose was broken and full of congealed blood and his left eye was a puffy black. But still he had not told them anything. Now he sensed instinctively he was in the presence of the Gestapo and he was really afraid.

Kranz looked at the two elderly cops who guarded the prisoner, his slanting eyes full of sadistic cunning. They nodded and began to prepare themselves for the interrogation.

'Now then,' Kranz said very carefully, 'I'm going to ask you three questions ... and I want you to answer them for me ... without trouble... Who are they? ... where were they going after they had carried out the murder?... Who was helping them?' He beamed down at the prisoner.

Sullenly Horst stared at his boots. He said nothing, his fingers twined together, as if he were trying to stop them trembling. Kranz lunged forward suddenly. He grabbed Horst by his long blond hair and, without warning he gave him a stinging blow across the side of the face that sent him reeling to the floor, retching and gasping.

Kranz pulled his sleeve down over his exposed cuff and nodded to the elderly cops. The two of them bent down, and with a grunt, hauled Horst back on to his stool

'Three questions, I asked you,' Kranz said softly.

Horst did not answer. But Kranz could see how he tensed his shoulder muscles, waiting for the next blow.

Kranz straightened up with a sigh, almost as if he were saddened by Horst's lack of understanding. 'Have you a pail and a broom?' he asked.

The senior cop looked at him, puzzled. 'Yes but—'

Kranz held up his hand for silence. 'Bring them please, would you?'

While they waited, the room was ominously silent, broken only by the ponderous ticking of the wall clock, and the tense breathing of the expectant prisoner. Moodily Kranz puffed at his cold cigar stump.

Finally the policeman returned with a white enamel pail and a stiff, wire-haired broom. Kranz grunted his approval and while Horst stared at him from under half-lowered lids, he put his big booted foot on the brush and tugged at the handle until it came free. He grunted, pleased with his own strength.

'All right,' he ordered, 'put the cuffs on him and tie him to the radiator over there.'

Obediently the two of them dragged Horst and his stool to the peeling white radiator.

Kranz strolled across slowly, as if he had all the time in the world and examined the man's hands tied securely to the radiator behind his back. 'Looks all right,' he exclaimed finally. 'Now put the pail on his head, please.'

The two cops looked at Kranz as if he were demented, but did as they were told.

Kranz took up the broom handle, measured his distance from the pail with it, then lashed it against the pail with all the force of his brutish shoulders. The metal pail sang. Horst's head snapped suddenly to the left and he was only prevented from being knocked off his stool by the handcuffs which cut cruelly into his wrists. The cops breathed out hard and looked at each other, their eyes full of shock.

'Take the pail off,' Kranz ordered.

Horst's face had turned livid purple. Blood was trickling blackly down from his clogged-up nostrils and bubbling out of his eardrums. His eyes were liquid with pain.

'Looks pretty – our tame Red,' Kranz laughed coldly. 'Do you know where I learned that trick?'

The elderly cops were used to the casual, rough treatment of prisoners by the German Police, but had never seen anything like this; they shook their heads silently.

'From old Commissar Schmidtheim of the Cologne Force. He's been looking at the potatoes from below for many a year now. But he always swore he could get an Egyptian mummy to confess by this little trick!' He chuckled again.

He turned to Horst again. 'All right, you heap of Communist shit, are you going to talk?'

Horst shook his head, biting his lips together to prevent himself from crying out with fear.

Kranz shrugged. 'All right, Communist, it's your funeral. Put the pail back on his head!'

Kranz began to beat the pail systematically, his breath coming in thick pleasurable gasps, while the cops stared at him and the prisoner in undisguised horror. Kranz no longer saw them. At that moment he was not even worried about whether or not his prisoner would talk. His sole concern was the pleasure which this inhuman act of punishment gave him: the thwack of the pole against the pail, the way the prisoner's body contracted each time, the sight of the crimson blood trickling down from under the pail on to his chest. But finally a protest from the senior cop that if he didn't stop soon, the prisoner might well die on him, forced Kranz back to his senses.

He dropped the pole with a clatter to the tiled floor already flecked with thick red gobs of blood. With fingers that trembled slightly, he took the cold stump of cigar out of his mouth. 'All right,' he breathed, his voice barely under control. 'Take it off!'

Horst's face was grotesquely puffed-up, an unrecognisable raw, red mess, from which the eyes peered through two narrow slits ringed with blood.

'Now listen. You're an unperson. You're as good as dead.' His voice grew warmer. 'Why not be sensible, lad? Why suffer any more?' He paused and made a great play of lighting his cigar. When he spoke again, he was sweet reasonableness itself. 'Why don't you save yourself from further hurt? Do you think they care about you now – those Tommies? They've blown and left you to face the music all on your lonesome. Now, son, what do you say, eh?'

'Go and shit in yer hat!' Horst croaked.

Angrily Kranz stubbed out his cigar on Horst's bloody cheek. There was a thin scream and the nauseous smell of burning flesh. 'All right, put the damn pail back on again!' he barked with rage. 'I'll make the bastard talk!'

Horst gave himself ten more blows of the pole before talking. He had grown used to Kranz's technique. After every five blows he would order the pail to be removed. Again he would ask the three questions, which Horst could barely hear with one eardrum already punctured and the other nearly gone. When he refused to answer, there would be some play with the cigar before it was stubbed out on his face. Then the beating would start once more. Ten ... nine ... eight ... seven ... six... Blow after blow. His teeth were beginning to fall out. His jaw was broken and one of his eyeballs felt as if it were full of hot glue. Both his lips were split and were bleeding badly. The ringing, terrible blows ceased. Through a red haze, he could see the brutal wavering face close to his. Dimly he recognised the questions. He didn't even care about them. His sole concern was to savour blessed freedom from the bone-shaking, excruciating thwack of the pole against the pail. He shook his head doggedly. The cigar came close. He could just see the red glow of its tip. As it ground into his face he could smell his own burning flesh, and screamed aloud. Darkness descended upon him once more, his nostrils filled with the salt-blood smell of the inside of the pail.

Five ... four ... three ... two ... one. As the pail was removed for the last time, he felt the warmth of the liquid beginning to trickle between his legs.

'Dirty bastard – he's pissed himself!' someone cried. He didn't care. He had done it – *he had held out!* Despite the searing pain of his mutilated face, he felt the satisfying glow of that achievement. Now he could sing; it no longer mattered. They had had time to get away; to change their plans. The pain could stop at last.

'I'll talk,' he croaked.

Kranz grinned triumphantly at the two cops, whose normally ruddy faces were now ashen. 'Didn't I tell you he would talk, *meine Herren?*' he boasted. 'They always talk in the end. Brave or cowardly, they always end up doing the same thing. No one can stand up to *that!*' Triumphantly, he kicked the pail and sent it clattering to the far end of the room. 'All right, Red turd, let's be having it. I've wasted enough time on you, as it is. Who are they?'

'American and British,' Horst quavered, spitting out a loose tooth.

'How do you know?' Kranz said. Behind him one of the cops picked up the pail and broom and opened the door to carry them out. Through the red haze in front of his eyes, Horst could dimly perceive the corridor and at the end, the tall window.

'I can … speak a little English… I listened at the hatch.'

'And where were they going after they had carried out their murder?' Kranz demanded.

Horst sucked the blood from his bottom lip before he answered, 'I think Metz… I listened the night they planned… They were going to use my barge to get to Metz.'

'Are you sure?'

'Yes.'

'Who was helping them beside you?'

'Can I have a piss before I go on?' Horst interrupted weakly. 'I must go ... otherwise I'll flood the floor.'

Kranz looked down at him contempt-uously. 'All right. *Wachtmeister,*' he snapped to the remaining cop, 'take the cuffs off him and take him out to clear his bladder. We don't want the dirty swine making any more mess.' He chuckled unpleasantly. 'It's always the same, once you've banged them around a bit, they always want to piss, just like the girls when you've stuck it into them for the first time!'

Kranz sat down on the stool and watched the cop escort the staggering, bedraggled prisoner down the corridor, urine dripping on the floor behind him. He puffed his cigar happily. He had had his pleasure and got the information he wanted. If that fat pig Meyer put in a good word for him, it might well mean promotion, and extra money was always welcome. Relaxed and pleased with himself, he followed the progress of the pathetic wreck of what had once been a man towards the latrine. Suddenly the prisoner straightened his shoulders. He pushed the surprised cop to one side. The policeman staggered against the wall, completely taken off guard and the next moment Horst was shambling down the corridor towards the two-metre-high window which provided it with light.

'*Stehenbleiben oder ich schiesse!*' bellowed the policeman, fumbling with his pistol holster.

With one last desperate burst of energy, the prisoner dived forward, crashing head-first through the window. By the time Kranz reached the shattered window Horst's body lay still, both arms flung out dramatically, one leg crumbled at an unnatural angle while his eyes stared unseeingly at the dawn sky.

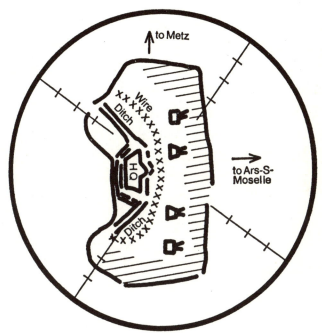

FORT DRIANT (September 1942)

ONE

By the end of their fourth day of hiding in the safe house of the Luxembourg Resistance, the Leg was beginning to haunt the exhausted Ultra men. On the first day after the beretted Resistance men had spirited them away to the little railwayman's cottage under the noses of the German occupiers, who had launched a massive search operation along the bank of the Luxembourg Moselle, it had been simply a curiosity.

They had woken up that first morning and stared at it as they lay there in their makeshift beds on the floor. A pair of trousers were draped over the little railwayman's own bed. One leg of them hung limp and normal; but the other was standing, well-pressed and straight, ending in the light tan shoe, which the railway clerk wore in his office at Wasserbillig Station. It contained the Leg.

They had asked Jean hesitantly how it had happened. He had not been in the least bitter. Indeed as they were later to find out he was proud of his leg, the result of the initial German artillery bombardment in 1940, when they had marched into the little Duchy. 'It makes me one of the few who have bled for Luxembourg,' he was wont to explain. 'Only fifty of us fell that day or were wounded. I was one of them. When the Duchess returns from London after the Boche is beaten, she will remember me, I have no doubt.' And he would add, his plump rosy features serious, 'and do you know what I'll do with the present she will undoubtedly give me then?'

'No, Jean.'

'I'll have an artificial leg made for every pair of trousers I possess. Then I'll stand them up in a row in my cupboard. You can't imagine what a time-wasting business it is to fit it into your trousers every morning when you're in a hurry to get to work.'

But by the fourth day, the Leg was beginning to get on their nerves. It was all right when Jean had it on. Then it was forgotten; it was part of the chubby, bespectacled little clerk. But when it was off, perched waiting at the end of his bed in the sole bedroom where they all slept on the floor, it exercised a morbid, irresistible fascination upon them. They couldn't take their eyes off it. As Spiv muttered to Cain more than once, 'I wouldn't be surprised if that bloody leg doesn't get up during the night when we're all sawing wood and walk around under its own ruddy steam!'

Yet despite the Leg, Cain had taken an immediate liking to the straight-faced little clerk who was daily risking his life by hiding them in his remote little cottage, while the enemy combed the whole area with a massive force of troops and police brought across the river from Germany. Thus it was that on the fourth day when the Leg and their cooped-up existence in the tight little cottage were beginning to play on their nerves, he decided – with Horst's unexpected loyalty on the tug in mind – to take Jean into his confidence.

While the other Ultra men silently sipped the fierce local plum schnapps in the little kitchen, he told him about as much of their mission as he felt safe to reveal.

Jean shrugged eloquently, his eyes sparkling intelligently behind his gold-rimmed glasses. 'They won't find you here, Major. But no wonder they launched such a search. I have never seen one of such magnitude since they took over in 1940. The Boche must want you badly.'

Cain looked glum. His wounded arm was paining him again. But it wasn't only that, it was the thought of their failure in Trier.

'Yes, Jean. By now they'll have him guarded by a whole damn battalion of troops down there in Trier, I'll be bound!'

Jean's eyes twinkled behind his glasses. 'You might be right that the General is being guarded by a battalion of troops, but not in Trier.'

Cain looked at him sharply and the others paused, with their glasses raised in mid-air. 'What do you mean?'

The one-legged Luxembourger chuckled. 'This very morning I had to process a movement order for a train from Wittlich in the Eifel, through Trier, Wasserbillig, Luxembourg City and on to the French border at Esch, where the French SNCF took over.'

'So?'

'Well, Major when the train came through this lunchtime, it was a troop train. But something about it struck me as strange. It was filled with troops of all arms and all ranks. SS officers and Wehrmacht NCOs, privates from the Luftwaffe, even a few pilots. There were many sailors too, although Wittlich is over six hundred kilometres from the sea. Don't you see? That troop train must have been carrying your Spanish volunteers, drawn from every arm of the German forces?'

'Jesus, Major,' Abel gasped, 'he must be right!'

Cain rapped his hook down on the scrubbed wooden table hard, 'Of course, of course! That must be it.' He looked at Jean. 'But what was the train's destination?'

'I don't know. After Esch, the French took it over. But it must be somewhere in the Occupied Zone. The Boche wouldn't dare send a troop train south of the Line.'

'Could you find out, Jean?' Cain asked urgently.

'Of course, but it would take a day or so. We Luxembourgers are slow, but we get there in the end, Major.'

They suffered another two days of the Leg, which, it now seemed to them, appeared to be resenting them, wanting them to be on their way. On the third day it had its way. Jean returned unexpectedly to the remote cottage at midday, bringing with him the exciting news that he had found the troop train's destination.

'Metz,' he announced proudly, easing the Leg on to a low stool, 'the train ended at Metz in Lorraine. And where those troops are, you'll find your celebrated *General der Luftwaffe* Meyer.'

'But Metz is big, Jean,' Cain objected. 'It must have at least a million or more citizens, and we're in no position to go around asking for the HQ of a German general.'

'I agree. But it is not as difficult as you think. No one in his right mind would set up his HQ in the barracks in the old part of the town. They are decrepit, three-hundred-year-old buildings with the grass growing on their roofs. Besides they are in the middle of the' – he hesitated and blushed – 'red light district. Your fastidious General wouldn't want to live and work there. My guess is,' he continued, 'that your General will establish himself in one of the forts.'

'Forts?' Cain queried.

'Yes, Metz was the most fortified city in Europe. It's surrounded by a network of two dozen of them in a line between the city and Thionville. The *Metz-Thionville Stellung*, the Boche call it. Some of them are pretty old, but the French kept them in good shape and after the Boche took over, they did the same. Now many of them are small and not suitable for an HQ.' He sucked his teeth for a moment thoughtfully. 'To my way of thinking, Major, only two forts come into question as an HQ – Fort Jeanne d'Arc and Fort Driant. Both are modern, highly secure against attacks by, say, the Underground, and have really modern communications systems. Yes,' he summed up, 'your target will be there for certain. Driant or Jeanne D'Arc – that's where you'll find him.'

During the next day, they familiarised themselves with the details of the two Metz forts, supplied promptly by the Luxembourg Resistance. Both of them stood apparently on hills, faded unobtrusively into the wooded landscape of the Metz suburbs. Enclosed by lines of barbed wire, bisected by moats and ringed concreted machine-gun emplacements, they were obviously very tough nuts to crack.

'Ay,' Mac grunted, after examining the rough sketches supplied by the Luxembourgers, 'it willna be easy to get into yon place.' He stabbed a thick finger at the centre of the sketch of Fort Driant. 'Look what we'll have to get through before we can make it to the headquarters! Bluidy infantry trenches running from here to here. Three concrete bunkers – the size of a wee *Queen Mary* and gun batteries everywhere. Why, man, we'd need a ton of P.E to blast our way in yon ruddy fort.'

'Can't you hush up, you bloody Scotch ray of sunlight!' Spiv snapped. 'You put sodding years on me, you do.'

Mac doubled his hamlike fist threateningly. 'What did ye say, ma wee man?'

Cain stepped in. 'All right, you two, save your fighting for the enemy. Things are bloody bad enough without having you trying to knock the stuffing out of each other. Let's have a bit of peace, so we can think this sod out.'

That evening after Jean had eaten his frugal supper and taken off the Leg with a sigh of relief, they put it to him. They were going to follow up his bit of inspired guesswork; they would move on to Metz as soon as possible. 'And bloody high time too,' Spiv muttered under his breath to no one in particular, eyeing the Leg standing firmly at the edge of the supper table, 'before that leg sends me off my rocker!' He shuddered eloquently.

Jean nodded, chewing happily on the last of his cold ham and egg pie.

'Do you think you could provide us with the requisite papers?' Cain asked, 'and perhaps some civvies? These we've got are pretty ropy to say the least.'

'Such things are no problem. The problem is that of transport.'

'How do you mean?'

'Well, the search is still going on for you in this area. The troops and the police are everywhere. The roads are impossible. All of them running south towards France have permanent road-blocks on them. They're out of the question.'

'What about automobiles?' Abel asked quickly.

Unconsciously Jean reached out one of his plump clerk's hands and patted the Leg as if for comfort, his ruddy face creased in thought. 'No, I don't think so,' he said finally. 'You were thinking of trying to break through the roadblocks – like in the gangsters films, eh? But there is no petrol and the top speed of the *gazogenes*' – he meant the wood-burning cars – 'is forty kilometres an hour downhill – with the wind behind them.' He chuckled. 'A barricade of matchwood would stop them.'

They fell silent for a while, each of them

preoccupied with his own thoughts, until Cain asked: 'What about by rail, Jean?'

'Yes, I had been thinking of that possibility myself. It is a short distance, exactly forty-eight minutes with a good driver, not one of those French layabouts,' he added hastily, making it clear that the good drivers had to be Luxembourgers. 'Your papers would safely see you by the French border check – the Boche leave it to them at the frontier with the Grand Duchy. The problem is getting on the train in the first place. They are everywhere at each station – even the smallest – between Wasserbillig and Luxembourg City, and everyone's papers are examined minutely, not only by the Boche but by those swine of collaborators. They'd spot you weren't Luxembourgers at once.'

'But can't we stage a distraction?' Cain asked, 'to give us enough time to get aboard and hide ourselves in the latrines. For instance, we might–'

Jean held up his hand imperiously. 'A distraction!'

Suddenly he slapped the Leg. 'Of course! We'll stage a *polterabend* specially for the Boche.'

'What's a *polterabend* when it's at home?' Spiv asked.

Jean smiled mysteriously. 'You'll find out tomorrow night, my friend. Now I think it is time for me and the Leg to go to sleep. It's

213

going to be a long day.'

Raising himself from the table, he picked up the Leg and, hopping happily to the bed, deposited it at the end. Spiv shuddered once again and closed his eyes.

TWO

The procession of cheering, sweating Luxembourg countryfolk swung round the corner and into the dusty, white village street towards the half-timbered house garlanded with green pines already beginning to wilt in the evening's heat. Beyond, at the country station, the four German guards, rifles slung over their shoulders, turned slowly to watch.

At the sight of the decorated house, the procession burst into song. In their midst the Ultra men, carrying beer bottles like the rest, waved them in unison, while taking in the sentries with anxious eyes. In thirty minutes the Trier-Metz train would stop for a few seconds at the station. When it left they had to be on it, sentries or no sentries.

Now shuttered windows were being opened along the street, baking in the summer heat, and heads, burned a brick-red by a long day in the fields, were thrust out to watch the proceedings. The band – a drummer, a trumpet player and a long dangling youth, armed with a trombone – burst unsteadily into some local air. At the windows the young girls giggled, while the matrons laughed knowingly at the obscenity of the words, heavy with peasant innuendo.

Next to a red-faced Mac, Jean hissed, 'The Boche are looking this way. Pretend to sing. Mime the words.'

'Not Mac,' Spiv whispered hastily, 'his voice would curdle the milk in them churns over there.'

'Sing!' Cain ordered. 'Sing, or I'll have the knackers off you, Spiv!'

They sang, as the procession flooded around the house belonging to the young couple, who were to be married the following Sunday at the onion-towered Baroque church across the way. As the song started to die away, the door, decorated in green and silver, opened to reveal the couple for whom this procession had been organised. The girl was a head taller than the groom-to-be, her massive bosom threatening to burst out of the tight silk of her Sunday dress. She said something to the young groom and he fumbled hastily with his flies. The crowd roared with laughter. Someone cupped his hands over his mouth and yelled: 'You're in a bit of a hurry, Emil, aren't you? You know yer supposed to wait for that till Sunday when the priest has made it legal!'

His sally was greeted with another burst of laughter and out of the corner of his eyes, Cain could see that the sentries who had obviously understood the thick local dialect, were smiling faintly too. It was a good sign; they were becoming more interested in the *polterabend,* the pre-marriage celebration, than in their duties. He glanced quickly at his watch. Twenty-five minutes to go!

At the door the undersized bridegroom, still flushed with embarrassment, picked up the heavy wicker basket of cheap crockery and deposited it in front of the crowd of well-wishers. 'Here, you are,' he announced, 'you can start now. The beer's ready for afterwards.' And with that he stepped back hastily out of the firing line. Not a moment too soon either.

A burly youth, his hair bleached to tow by the summer sun, picked up a plate and hurtled it at the nearest wall. It shattered there to the accompaniment of excited cheers of the crowd, who knew that after this part of the ceremony was over, there would be free beer and the fierce local plum schnapps for the rest of the evening till the curfew forced them off the streets. Another youth picked up a cup and whirling it like an American baseball pitcher hurled it at the wall, where it shattered like a shell exploding. Again there were cheers. But the first two men's efforts obviously did not please the burly woman, with whom Jean had planned the operation that morning.

'What a lot of wet tails,' she jeered contemptuously. 'And you lot call yourselves men! Now then let a weak woman show you how it is done!'

As had been planned, the crowd parted to let her get to the crockery basket. Deliberately she rolled up her sleeves to reveal two mighty hams, red to the elbow, where they had been exposed to the sun in the fields. She spat carefully on each of her mighty hands like a workman preparing to undertake a particularly hard task. She bent with a grunt, her back to the Germans, her short skirt riding high up her legs as she did so. Carefully she selected a cup, while the sentries' eyes bulged at the spectacle offered them.

Jean nudged Cain. 'They're biting,' he whispered urgently, 'start moving round the crowd. They'll keep you covered.'

'Right.'

Slowly, casually they began to edge their way closer to the station. The sentries stared entranced at the woman's naked behind, as she still pondered over her selection. The fat woman hurtled the first cup at the wall. It exploded there, shattering pieces of china everywhere. At the door the watching couple ducked hurriedly as the fragments hissed by them like shrapnel. The crowd cheered with delight. 'Good for you, Eddi!' someone yelled. 'But watch you don't split yer knickers!'

Eddi, whose ample charms were well known to most of the village youths, beamed, revealing a gap-toothed smile and yelled, 'I can't, George. I never wear 'em, as you well know from last week behind the barn!'

Her sally was greeted by another burst of delighted laughter as she bent down again.

'God love a duck,' Spiv breathed as he saw for the first time what she was revealing. 'Get a load of that, Major – she's cut herself already and not even begun to shave yet!'

'Shut yer filthy Cockney mouth,' Mac grunted threateningly, carefully avoiding, with his one good eye, the expanse of rounded naked flesh. 'Have ye no other thought in yer mind than that?'

'Ner, what do you want me to do – tie it to me ruddy leg all the time?'

Cain gave him a shove in the ribs. 'Move on, we're nearly there now.'

The sentries were absorbed now in the spectacle. In a minute the youths at the edge of the crowd would begin to hand them bottles of beer already being passed out by the groom, content now that his matrimonial happiness had been secured by the breaking of the china.

Jean pressed Cain's good hand; there were sudden tears behind his gold-rimmed glasses. 'Till after the war!' he whispered.

'Till after the war, Jean,' Cain answered. 'And I'll personally buy you a new leg for each suit of clothes you possess.'

Jean grinned through his tears, then he turned back into the cheering crowd.

'Okay, now!' Cain ordered.

The first sentry had already accepted the stubby bottle of powerful Luxembourg beer. With his heavy helmet pushed to the back of his head, he was guzzling it gratefully, not taking his eyes of Eddi. Behind him his comrades were reaching out their hands for bottles too, with urgent cries of 'ich auch, *bitte!*' They did not even see the four poorly-clothed civilians who edged behind them into the shadows at the entrance of the village station.

The ticket collector, who had been informed by Jean of what was going on, quickly clipped their tickets and whispered conspiratorially: 'The up-platform. It'll be in in five minutes. There's nobody about. *Bonne chance!*'

'Thank you,' they replied and passed through the barrier on to the platform, bare of anything save a few parcels and a leather sack of mail, obviously intended for the capital, Luxembourg City. 'Spread out–'

Cain never finished the command. A heavy-set man in German uniform, with the silver plate of the *Feldgendarmerie* around his neck, suddenly emerged from the *pissoir* fumbling with his flies. He spotted them at once. Perhaps he had even heard Cain's order in English. They never found out. But his reaction was spontaneously suspicious.

'Hey,' he demanded gruffly, 'who are you? Have you been checked yet?' His hand dropped to his pistol.

It was the worst move he could have made. Mac reacted instinctively; he grabbed the hayfork which was standing at the wall next to the latrine and lunged. The high-pitched scream of agony was drowned by the train's whistle as it rounded the bend. The German's big hands flew to his chest. The Field Gendarme's legs started to sag. But he wasn't finished yet and Cain realised with a flash of fear that he only needed to shout once and the sentries would come running.

'Finish him off, Mac,' he cried urgently. *'Quick!'*

Mac needed no prompting. With a thick grunt, he stabbed the hayfork into the German's guts. The cruel steel prongs sank in deeply, right to the guard. Mac forced him into the *pissoir,* where his dying cries of agony would be deadened by the thick walls.

Abel turned his head, sickened by the naked brutality, while Mac brought up the fork again and again and stabbed it down convulsively at something which lay crumbled and twitching on the urine-wet floor of the *pissoir*. And then it was over. Mac dropped the fork with a clatter on to the wet tiles. Weakly, he staggered out of the stinking *pissoir*, while Cain and Spiv, galvanised into action, grabbed the parcels and the sack of mail and scattered them over the blood-stained crumpled body in a rough-and-ready attempt to conceal it for at least a couple of hours.

The rusty great locomotive was beginning to steam slowly into the little country station, towing a long line of battered carriages behind it. They caught a glimpse of the sign painted in white letters along the length of the locomotive *'Wheels Roll for the Victory'* and the hated swastika, and then the train came to a protesting, squeaky halt. Swiftly Cain pushed Mac in front of him. 'Come on – quick,' he urged, as listless faces stared out at them from the wooden-seated compartments. They passed a carriage marked *'Fuer Wehrmachtsangehorige'*. German soldiers looked at them from within it. That was no good. The next carriage was marked 'For Mothers With Children Only'. That was out too. Up front the locomotive was beginning to release steam noisily, its metal sides vibrating like a trained racing dog trembling to be released from the leash. Then they spotted what they were looking for – a first-class carriage, occupied solely by a slant-eyed burly man in a long leather coat, with Gestapo written all over him.

'In there,' Cain urged. 'Nobody'll give us trouble sitting in the same compartment as that bloke.'

A few seconds later they were safely ensconced in the first-class compartment, opposite the Gestapo man. Outside, the guard waved his metal disc and yelled *'Alles einsteigen!'* A whistle blew. The train shuddered. Its wheels rattled violently. Slowly it began to move out of the little station. They were on their way.

Opposite them, the man with the cunning, slanting eyes gave them a casual look; then *Oberkommissar* Kranz closed his eyes and drifted off back into the sleep which had been broken by the stop at the Godforsaken Luxembourg station.

THREE

For a moment in his rage, Kranz forgot Meyer's rank. 'Look,' he tapped the photo of the murdered Field Gendarme, sprawled out in dramatic savagery on the floor of the latrine, 'look what they did, the Tommy bastards!'

'But my dear man,' the General objected,

'how can you know it was them!'

'Oh, I know, I know it! It has to be them. And I *actually* passed the place where it happened on my way here to Metz, would you believe that!'

'What a shock that must have been for your sensitive soul,' said Meyer ironically.

'And why do you think they killed that soldier, General?' he asked challengingly. 'I'll tell you. Because they were trying to break through our cordon to get on the Metz train. Great crap on the Christmas Tree!' he breathed with sudden urgency, as the thought flashed into his brain, 'I might well have travelled with them for all I know!' Kranz looked down at the General, his mouth opened incredulously, cigar stump dangling precariously from his thick lower lip.

Meyer put down his fountain pen and stared up at the Gestapo man from behind his desk. 'But Kranz, what has all this got to do with me? You know how damned busy I am with the move here and everything?'

'Yes, yes. *Herr General.*' Kranz remembered suddenly to whom he was speaking and pulled himself together. 'I am sorry. But I felt it was my duty to warn you that there would be another attempt on your life.'

'Impossible!' Meyer exclaimed. 'Now come on, Kranz, do you seriously think that four Tommy terrorists could break into this place and try to kill me? *In Fort Driant?*'

Without waiting for an answer from Kranz, he rose ponderously to his feet and walked over to the illuminated map of the great Fort on the wall of his underground office. 'Just look at this map of the place and its environments, will you?' He tapped the wall with the knuckles of his pudgy, beringed right hand like a lecturer attracting the attention of an audience. 'Fort Driant belongs to the outer ring of the Metz fortresses. The main defences consist of four casemates with reinforced concrete walls, two metres thick – and here, where we are now, the central fort in the shape of a pentagon. From here to there we are connected by underground tunnels. If that weren't enough, the central fort is surrounded by a dry moat, twenty metres wide and ten metres deep, with wings extending out on either side. That is covered by barbed wire to a depth of twenty-five metres. Finally the whole lot is guarded by a battalion of infantry – say some eight hundred men.' He paused and looked directly at the Gestapo man. 'Now, I repeat, Kranz, do you seriously think that they could pull it off under such circumstances?'

Kranz hesitated. He stared back at the General, his face glistening with sweat in the warmth of the artificially lit, windowless underground office.

Meyer pushed home his advantage. 'I

sleep here, I eat here and I probably won't see daylight again for over a week the way things are going at the moment, with the pressure of work.' He chuckled throatily. 'Fort Driant, if you like, is a nice big concrete coffin protecting these well-nourished bones of mine.'

'I understand, General,' Kranz said finally. 'But those Tommies are cunning shits. You must admit that the events of the past week have shown that. Haven't they evaded the security forces of the Reich time and again? For instance, what if they recruited the local Resistance and made an all-out attack on this place?'

'They would be slaughtered in their hundreds on that belt of barbed wire up there – and they would not even see the men who had done the slaughtering.'

'What about poison gas?' Kranz asked, casting around wildly for something which would make the General take the danger more seriously. 'If they pumped some deadly gas down your ventilation system, eh?'

Meyer chuckled easily, his flabby jowls trembling as he did so. 'No problem, Kranz. The air conditioning is automatically filtered and would prevent any known poison gas from penetrating the ventilating system. Besides, how would they know which shaft leads to this particular office and whether I would be in it at that particular time?' He chuckled again. 'No my dear policeman, those Tommies of yours would have to be the Holy Ghost himself to be able to get into Fort Driant. Now don't worry. I promise you that I shall remain underground for the next few days, and that while I am down here I am one hundred per cent safe.'

General der Luftwaffe Meyer frowned as he thought of the reason for his decision to remain working at his desk, twelve, fourteen hours a day. The day before he had received a long, coded message – via the Enigma – from the *OKW* in which the High Command revealed it now had detailed information that the Anglo-Americans were far advanced in their preparations for an attack somewhere in the Mediterranean. Admiral Canaris's *Abwehr* agents posted along the coast opposite Gibraltar, had reported a tremendous military build-up on the Rock, and Air Reconnaissance had spotted large concentrations of troop transports, complete with landing craft, in several British ports. Furthermore, agents in the United States had reported that a news blackout had been clamped down on the American east coast: a sure sign that large-scale troop movements were taking place in the area.

Obviously the balloon was soon to go up and by then he must have his own contingency plan perfect and coordinated with the Wehrmacht's plan to occupy Vichy France, in case the Allies landed in Southern France. Hence his presence with his volunteers in Metz, the most suitable rail and air head for a quick thrust to Seville through the Army units which would be advancing into the Unoccupied Zone of France at the same moment.

'So, *mein lieber Kranz,* I feel you are concerning yourself unnecessarily about my safety down here in the bowels of the earth,' Meyer concluded, sitting down behind his massive desk and picking up his pen again with an air of finality.

Kranz nodded slowly, 'Perhaps you're right, *Herr General.* But I have a request.'

'Yes?'

'Have I your permission to stay here in Fort Driant for a while? I have my superior's permission.'

'Be my guest, Kranz,' Meyer said expansively, shaking the pen to make the ink flow. 'But I am quite certain that your services will not be required. Take it from me – Fort Driant is impregnable.'

It was a conclusion to which the Ultra men too were slowly coming. All that afternoon they had been reconnoitring the outskirts of the great fort while pretending to pick the mushrooms which dotted the fields surrounding the bald-topped hill on which it rested.

Nearly 1,200 feet in height and fringed sparsely by trees, it dominated the whole area, the only approach the white-gleaming concrete road running up the main works from the little river village of Ars-sur-Moselle down in the valley below.

Now, squatting in the shade of the thick patch of wood on the south-west slope of the hill, they munched disconsolately on the *baguettes* and hard cheese, bought in Metz with the money Jean had given them. In the end it was Abel who gloomily broke the heavy silence.

'That goddam hill dominates the whole area, that's for sure. From up there anyone down here must stick out like a flea on a shorn sheep's back.'

'Then we go in under the cover of darkness,' Mac growled aggressively, mouth full of bread and cheese.

'Come off it!' Spiv objected. 'How? Look at that ruddy barbed wire everywhere. And I bet my bottom dollar that them trenches is full of squareheads at night too.'

'What about the main entrance?' Abel suggested hopefully, brightening up a little. 'Coming up from Ars-sur-Moselle by the supply road?'

'There'll be a password and probably sentries posted in those little pillboxes on both sides,' Cain said despondently. 'The whole works. We wouldn't have a cat's chance in hell, I'm afraid.'

Again the four of them fell into a heavy silence broken only by the faint bleating of the sheep cropping the grass up above them, and Mac's steady munching on the tough French bread. After a while Cain rose wearily to his feet and standing with his back to the others, he urinated – in case anyone was watching them through binoculars – and surveyed the Fort once again. He could make out the great concrete gun casemates easily. Obviously the General they had come so far to kill would not have his HQ anywhere, it would be in the five-sided earthwork on the top of the hill, guarded both by a large dry, anti-tank ditch and a thick, continuous belt of concertino wire, mixed with barbed wire. That would be the place all right. But how in hell's name were they going to get into it?

Fastening his flies angrily, Cain snapped, 'All right, that's enough for today. It's too risky to hang about any longer. It's getting dark and perhaps they send out patrols after dusk.' He sniffed and looked at Spiv still chewing contentedly on his bread. 'Let's get ourselves back to those disreputable establishments which you found for us to lay our weary heads.'

Spiv's face brightened. 'It's not our heads we want to lay there, sir,' he said.

'Oh, shut up, Spiv,' Cain snapped miserably. 'Come on, let's get back to Metz.'

Wearily they started to shuffle off down the road towards the great Lorraine city.

It had been Spiv's idea to spend the nights in various of the *maisons de passe,* which dotted the crumbling, grey-stone area of the old city around the ancient Gothic cathedral. In their two years of occupation, the Germans had not closed France's brothels and as the *maisons de passe,* where a man could take a girl at any time of night or day for a couple of hours, were roughly in the same class, they had not been closed either. More important, the owners of such establishments did not ask for papers or registration, and they were free from the midnight searchers instituted in regular hotels by the Germans and their helpers in the French Police. There they would book a room – no questions asked – and go upstairs saying they were soon expecting a girl to rest on the dirty bed for a couple of hours before moving on again.

But as they picked their way through the darkening streets filled with the bicycles, the occasional French car belching flame from its producer gas container, German trucks and the velo-taxis, cycle-powered taxis driven by husky, powerfully muscled young men, a miserable Cain did not fancy settling in for the night yet in some flea-ridden *maison de passe.*

Instead he said, 'It's a *jour avec,* isn't it. Let's go and get a drink, eh?'

The others needed no urging after their failure of the afternoon. Yesterday had been a *jour sans,* when, by order of the German occupiers, only soft drinks were served in the many bistros of the area. Today, as on every alternative day of the week, the bars could tender real alcohol.

They filed silently in to one of the many bars which lined the cobbled market place dominated by the Cathedral. They took up their positions near the rear entrance so that they could view unobserved the rest of the sleazy establishment in the mirror which ran the length of the bar.

Abel ordered *vermouth cassis* for himself and Cain, and the fierce local *mirabelle* for Spiv and Mac who disdained 'yon sweet stuff, meant for a lot of frilly-knickered old wives'. Now the four of them sat there in gloomy silence, sipping their drinks, and watching the other customers. A beretted businessman with a face like a petulant Clemenceau, boasting loudly to the bartender of the ten kilos of butter he had managed to pick up on the black market 'for a song'. A burly old man, with a walrus-moustache and the medal ribbons in his right lapel of the First War veteran, big red hands clamped over his walking stick held between his legs, staring blankly, glass untouched in front of him. A dark Italianate-looking young man with long sidechats slashed down each side of his narrow face, trying to get a young blonde drunk with *Diabolo Menthe,* sliding his pale, soft hand up her skirt from time to time when he thought no one was watching.

Cain stared at them in scarcely concealed disgust. These were Abel's little people, now conquered by a brutal oppressor. But did any of them look particularly resentful or oppressed? He didn't think so by the expressions on their easy-going faces. Most of them seemed to have forgotten that a life-or-death struggle was being waged, supposedly on their behalf, over half the globe.

Abel seemed to be able to read his thoughts. 'They all look so normal,' he whispered. 'You know, Cain – like one of those pre-war French movies by Rene Clair? *Le Jour se Lève* – something like that?'

Cain nodded but said nothing. Grimly he forced himself to dismiss his feelings of despair and concentrate on the problem at hand. Before they went their various ways to spend the night in their particular *maison de passe,* he would love to have worked out a plan of operations. But however much he racked his brain, he could not seem to find a way of surmounting the fact that Fort Driant was one hundred per cent impregnable.

It was as he stared gloomily once more into his vermouth, that they struck lucky. Just as the cross-eyed bartender was beginning to fetch the blackout shutters from behind the bar, a long camouflaged staff car slid into view in the big fly-blown mirror. For what seemed a long time, Cain did not take in the significance of the metal flag it was flying at its bonnet, as the car edged its way slowly through the crowded square. Then he recognised it. Hastily he nudged Abel.

'Hey, take a look at the car. Quick!'

Abel and the others threw a swift glance at the mirror, just as the staff car disappeared out of sight. It was empty save for the uniformed chauffeur concentrating on the task of getting safely through the cyclists who swarmed everywhere on their way home after a hard day in Metz's engineering works. But it was time enough for them to recognise the vehicle they had last seen on that fateful night in Trier outside Madame Lola's.

'Gee, it's his!' Abel exclaimed excitedly. 'It's General Meyer's automobile!'

'Och, man, will ye no keep your voice down!' Mac growled urgently, as the bartender looked up from his blackouts to stare at them for a moment.

The four of them pretended to be occupied with their drinks and the Frenchman concentrated on his work again.

'Well, what do you make of it?' Cain whispered a few moments later when he was out of earshot. 'What in heaven's name is General Meyer's car doing in this disreputable part of town, eh?'

It was Spiv who provided the answer. He winked and thrust his thumb between two forefingers in the Continental fashion. 'That,' he said. 'Or do I need to draw you a flipping picture?'

FOUR

Naturally it was Spiv who found the place for them in the end. A few words of fractured French with the owner of the *maison de passe*, where he had spent the previous night; several knowing winks on Spiv's part and a thin leer from the Frenchman; a grubby crumpled one-hundred-franc note passed furtively across the counter, and they had the address they sought.

Now as they walked through the blackout towards the *Porte des Allemands*, where the establishment was located, Spiv explained the matter with all the aplomb of a professional psychologist, if not his vocabulary. 'You see when a bloke gets to a certain age and wants a bit of the other, he starts preferring the young tarts. Perhaps some of the old geezers want to get in at the ground floor, if yer follow me? Get there while it's still nice and juicy and fresh.'

Mac snorted indignantly, but Spiv ignored him.

'But I think for most of them, they prefer the young tarts – you know, about fourteen or fifteen – because they won't laugh at them if they can't get their pecker up, like an experienced judy would. Besides if he can't get it up, he can always give the young tart a cheap thrill because she wouldn't know there were better things to be had.' They stopped to let a patrol of German soldiers march by, a sudden reminder of just how precarious their position was in the blacked-out French city.

'Square-headed bastards!' Mac cursed and spat into the dirty gutter, as they moved off again towards the spiked outline of the *Porte des Allemands*' towers, silhouetted against the purple of the summer night sky.

'So, I thought,' Spiv continued, 'wherever you get a big place and older geezers with plenty of dough – yer know what they say – a fat wallet always makes for instant love – there'd be a place that would cater for them, the kind who likes the young stuff.'

'Jail bait, you mean?' Abel queried.

'Yer could call it that. Cradle-snatching we'd call it in proper English like we speak back home. Anyhow that's how I came up with the idea.'

'You're a genius, Spiv,' Cain said, as they halted facing the address the Frenchman had given them.

'Yes,' Spiv answered modestly, 'I allus thought I'd a bit more of the old grey matter than most folk.'

'Och, away with yer, man!' Mac snapped. 'Come on, let's get on with it.'

In single file they began to cross the road towards the still, grey-stone eighteenth-century house which, as the Frenchman had put it catered 'for elderly gentlemen with special needs'.

Madame Zaza, plump, peroxided and shrewd, eyed them suspiciously as they sat opposite her in the over-heated, red-lit parlour.

'Zaza feels,' she said in a curiously hoarse voice, 'you are not the kind of person that this establishment usually – er – caters for.'

Abel, who spoke the best French of them all, took up the challenge. 'Madame,' he asked, taking the bull by the horns, 'are you a patriot?'

The forty-year-old brothel-keeper with the firm strong face, marred only by thick sensual red lips looked at him, half-amused, half-serious. 'Zaza thinks she is. But Zaza is also a businesswoman.' She shrugged swiftly.

236

'One has to make compromise.'

'That is sufficient for me, Madame,' Abel retorted. 'I need your help.'

'What kind of help? Zaza *sells* only one type of help.'

'Madame, this evening you probably received a visit from a German – a German soldier, driving a big automobile.'

Zaza looked at him shrewdly, her dark eyes trying to assess the handsome young man. 'Yes, it is true. Zaza did receive a visit from such a German earlier this evening. It was a surprise for Zaza and her little friends. You see the Boc' – she corrected herself hastily – *'Messieurs les Allemands* do not usually have much need for Zaza's specialised services. They are young men, virile, with no need of any – let us say – expert assistance.'

Cain was inwardly amused. Zaza was a card. Not only was she a brothel-owner, a lesbian too by the look of her, but also the type of woman who might well give a thrill of pleasure to any masochist in need of 'help'.

'Do you know who that soldier represented?' Abel continued.

Zaza shrugged. 'Zaza never asks too many questions. If this particular answer is good,' she rubbed imaginary money between her nicotine-stained thumb and forefinger, 'there is usually little need for any further questions.'

'Well, I shall tell you, Madame. That Boche was the chauffeur to a certain German General Meyer,' he hesitated momentarily, 'a man we have come a long way to kill, Madame.'

'*What* did you say, young man?'

Hastily Abel explained what their mission was in Metz, ending with a bald statement of their helplessness. 'Without your aid, Madame, we cannot do anything. We have failed. Madame, the success of our operation lies in your hands.'

For what seemed a long time there was a heavy silence in the room. A couple of times Zaza looked down at her heavy, square-nailed hands, as if she were considering Abel's statement literally while Cain watched her anxiously.

Finally she spoke, picking her words with great care, as if she were facing a courtroom full of lawyers. 'You see, Madame Zaza has to earn a living. That is understood, isn't it?'

They nodded.

'But Madame Zaza has a brain and a heart too.' She tapped her plump left breast with her brown, square-nailed finger. 'We are not mercenary like your average Frenchwoman, and we are not as weak-kneed like your average Frenchman. We have guts!'

Again they nodded encouragingly, but said nothing.

'*Hein,* so we do not like the Boche. We do

not like to see them in our cafes, in our streets, even at the Cathedral on a Sunday when we go to mass. They are an offence for us. But as I say, we see little of them in our business. *Alors,* when one of them came to make inquiries this evening, we didn't like it. But we hid our dislike and thought of the money, what else could we do? After all we are nothing but a weak frail woman.'

Spiv bit his bottom lip to prevent himself from laughing.

'But how can Zaza help – without endangering herself and her little darlings?' She held up her finger warningly. 'That is if she decided to help you.'

Abel seized his chance eagerly. 'Did the chauffeur want you to arrange girls to be sent up to Fort Driant, Madame? Which girls and when? What were the arrangements–'

'*Oh, la la!*' She put up her hands, as if to ward him off. 'So many questions, young man! So many. Why not let Zaza's little darlings tell you themselves. And you can trust them,' she added, seeing the look of alarm in their eyes. 'Zaza has reared them all personally ever since she accepted them into her service. They are loyal to Zaza, to the death. You,' she pointed to Mac, 'with the ugly face and the windowpane in his eye, pull that bellrope behind you.'

Even Mac could not resist the imperious

command. Flushed and muttering to himself, he tugged the bellrope.

A moment later the twin doors opened to admit Zaza's little darlings. The first one, who couldn't have been a day older than thirteen, came in boldly, her budding breasts thrust out provocatively against the sheer silk nightie she was wearing. The second was hesitant, yet knowing, dressed like a French schoolgirl down to the very short skirt and white kneesocks, although she wore extremely high heels. The third was completely naked save for a short white chemise which did not hide the soft curve of her white belly, running down to the faint brown powder puff of her pubic hair which she thrust out blatantly at them. Another two followed, dressed in long children's flannel nightgowns, their faces devoid of any make-up, their hair worked up into tight white cloth curlers so that they looked as if they had just got out of bed.

Zaza gazed at them fondly and then her face hardened again. 'Girls, you are forgetting yourselves,' she rapped sternly. 'There are gentlemen present.'

Like a bunch of convent girls, they curtsied demurely, while Mac's face flushed beetroot and Spiv's eyes seemed to be about to burst from their sockets.

Abel licked his suddenly dry lips and tried to take his eyes off the first girl's rosy-tipped breasts, nuzzling against the sheer silk. 'You said, Madame, that – er – your girls would answer our questions?'

She nodded. 'Marieclair – Rosemarie,' she snapped. 'What did the Boche want?'

They explained in breathless little girl voices, tinged with a huskiness affected presumably for sexual reasons, that Meyer wanted their 'services' for the coming evening.

'At Fort Driant?' Cain asked.

'Yes,' answered Marieclair, the one in the sheer silk nightdress. 'Tomorrow night punctually at nine, the Boche will collect us in his car.'

Cain bit his bottom lip, even forgetting the little girls' wanton nakedness, as a plan began to form in his mind.

They spent the next hours hotly discussing his rough-and-ready in the little room which Zaza had placed at their disposal after dismissing the girls and promising her help so long as it wouldn't endanger 'Zaza and her little darlings'.

'So you see,' Cain urged, feeling more and more confident that they could pull it off, 'we could use that car to get right into the Fort without the least bit of trouble. After all, what sentry would dare to stop the General's car, especially when it was driven by his chauffeur and contained a special cargo – Zaza's girls –

about which the General would be very annoyed to have questions asked?'

'Yes, yes, man, I understand that well enough,' Mac objected. 'The car's a splendid idea. But think straight, man, we can no very well drive in openly with the chauffeur up front, can we now?'

'We won't, Mac,' Cain answered. 'The boot of that Horch is big enough to hold the four of us – and then some.'

'But how do you propose to get us into that boot – and what if it's locked, eh?' Abel asked.

'I've thought of that one, too, Abel,' Cain replied. 'What do you think that chauffeur must feel like, fetching and carrying pretty young girls for the General all the time?'

'Like me,' Spiv answered the question for him and gave a mock groan, 'like a spare penis at a wedding. Always the bridesmaid and never the bride!'

The others laughed softly and upstairs the rhythmic squeak of the bedsprings seemed to lend emphasis to their spectator role here in Madame Zaza's establishment.

'Yes,' Cain said eagerly, 'he wouldn't object to getting a little something himself. Why couldn't Madame Zaza delay him for expressly that purpose? He could always explain it somehow or other later to the General. And in the meantime we could get ourselves hidden in the Horch.'

'But what if the chauffeur stops the car way off the General's quarters, somewhere nice and bright for everyone to see us emerge from the Horch?' Abel asked. 'I mean I don't want to knock your plan, Cain. But one has to take that into consideration, and there are only four of us against what looked to me a darn battalion of Krauts.'

'I get your point. But I have the feeling that the General wouldn't like to have too many witnesses to his little pecadillos. Would you, if you indulged in the kind of perversion that he seems to enjoy? No, it's my firm conviction that he will want the girls delivered as discreetly and as close to his quarters as possible.' Cain dropped his voice and looked at them hopefully. Upstairs the creaking springs had reached a crescendo. 'What do you say – is it on?'

One by one they nodded their heads in silent agreement, all save Spiv, whose mind seemed elsewhere, perhaps on the exciting action taking place in the bedroom above their heads. 'Well, Spiv, what do you say?' Cain asked finally.

'I've only one question, sir. I'm sure we'll get into that ruddy Fort all right. But,' he looked at Cain mournfully, 'are yer so bloody sure, sir, that we're ever gonna get out again?'

Despite his unpleasant forebodings, Spiv

was not going to miss the splendid opportunities offered him by Madame Zaza's establishment. As he told himself while he waited there for Madame Zaza to leave Marieclair's bedroom in the small hours of the morning, 'We'd rather fuck than fight.'

Three hours later he was ready to leave. Giving Marieclair a last hug, he grabbed his clothes and tiptoed towards the door. Suddenly he stopped and turned to stare at her, sprawled out in naked, exhausted abandon on the rumpled, sweat-stained bed. 'Listen, Marieclair, I've got something for you,' he said softly in his best French accent.

The teenager sat up lazily, her hands over her budding pink breasts, her mercenary instincts aroused.

'Not that, missus. That's died a natural death, thank you very much,' he said in English, pleased with the success of the evening. 'This,' he responded in her own language. He reached in his pocket and brought out the flat metal object, which he had stolen from Mac on the off-chance and which he knew was Churchill's Toyshop's latest invention.

'What is it?' she pouted disappointed when she saw that it wasn't the valuable present she expected.

Swiftly he explained its purpose.

'But what do you want me to do with it, Spiv?' she asked, drawing out the Spiv as if it had a couple of extra vowels.

'Take it with you tomorrow night when you go to visit the General with Rosemarie.' He hesitated an instant, as if he were scared of his own vision of what might happen in Fort Driant, 'and keep it with you the whole time in case it might be needed.'

She shrugged eloquently. 'But where shall I hide it, Spiv? The Boche, he will expect me to be naked, *hein*. They always do, the old men. And a naked woman has no pockets.'

Spiv winked at her solemnly and picked up his shoes. 'Oh, yes she has you know, darling. The way that old boy has trouble with his pecker, he'll never find out, will he?'

FIVE

Cautiously Cain began to raise the heavy door to the boot. It was now over five minutes since the heavy hobnails of the chauffeur and the light, quick high-heeled step of the two girls had died away. Now, with luck, they would be alone. He peeped out through the crack. The Horch had been parked in what looked like a large underground bunker, lit by a faint yellow light.

'Well?' Spiv whispered behind him.

'It looks okay,' he whispered back.

'Then for God's sake, let's get out and chance it. If I stay in here a minute more close to this great hairy Jock, I'll have to marry the bugger.'

Cain laughed softly and raising the lid higher, crept out. Gratefully he stretched his limbs while the others did the same.

A couple of half-tracks were parked against one wall. A little further on there was a line of little carts like those used in mines. Cain told himself that they were probably for moving heavy shells below in the casemates, or for bringing up supplies. Beyond them, he saw what looked like a large glass cage, with a little slotted window-panel for talking through: the kind of thing he remembered from factory entrances in France. Otherwise the underground bunker was empty. So far, so good.

'All right,' he whispered, 'off we go.'

As quietly as they could, they began to cross the bunker. Even so, it seemed to Cain they were making a hell of a noise, the slightest sound magnified by the great echoing underground chamber. Anxiously he eased his pistol, which he stuck in his belt just below the jacket, into a more con-venient position, though he hoped to heaven he would not have to use it.

They had almost reached the glass cage structure, when there was a soft hiss. 'Someone farted!' Spiv whispered urgently.

They froze. On any other occasion that too human sound would have been simply ludicrous, vulgarly funny. But not now. For them it was a frightening signal of alarm. Cain controlled his heart, which was beating like a triphammer.

'I'll check it out,' he hissed, 'cover me.'

Half-crouched, he tiptoed the rest of the way. Taking a deep breath, he raised his head gingerly over the sill.

Half a dozen German soldiers in various stages of undress were sprawled out on the floor on their straw mattresses. A couple of them were already asleep, mouth opened stupidly as they snored. One was sitting on his bunk, cleaning a carbine with the dedication of the ambitious young soldier trying very hard to make corporal. The rest, still in their grey uniform jackets were playing *skat* on the floor, cigarettes stuck in the corners of their mouths, eyes wrinkled up against the smoke. Cain thought swiftly. Only one of then had a weapon in his hands; the rest of their weapons were neatly lined up in the rack in the corner. They could be taken. But it only needed the earnest, red-faced private with the rifle to loose off a single shot and the whole damned garrison would be alarmed. There had to be another way.

'It's some sort of guardroom,' he informed the others in a tense whisper. 'There's half a dozen of the buggers in there. Only one of them is armed. Easy meat. But that one feller could just well be the one to bugger us up.'

'Judo?' Abel suggest hopefully. 'We're all familiar with it.'

Cain shook his head.

'Major, what about this?' It was Mac and he was holding up what looked like a Parker fountain pen.

'What is it?'

'The latest toy from the Toyshop. Still on the secret list.'

'I asked you what it is, Mac,' Cain repeated.

'Gas,' Mac announced grimly.

Abel flashed him a look of fear. 'You mean some sort of knock-out gas?' he demanded.

Mac shook his head. 'Poison gas – effective fifteen seconds.'

'You must be joking – we don't use poison gas in the west, Mac.'

Mac nodded solemnly. 'Its use is being considered at the highest level in London and Washington, Abel. We've been making these pens at the Toyshop for several months now.'

Abel looked at Cain almost pleadingly. 'Cain, in these last few weeks, you – we – have done some terrible things. But not … not that!'

Cain looked at him coldly. 'You – we – will

all do a lot worse before this damned war is over, Abel. Now there's no way. It's either them or us. If we win the war, their leaders will be put on trial as war criminals. If it's the other way around, it'll be ours – and us. So let's ensure that we win, whatever the means.'

Abel's gaze filled with horror. 'God, I know you're a hard bastard, Cain. But not even you can mean that! Why that's the logic of ... of the devil. I'm not going to–'

But it was already too late; Mac had taken the matter into his own big hands. Pushing Abel to one side so that he was caught off his guard and stumbled to his knees, he raised the glass window and dropped in the pen.

Throwing caution to the winds, they raced after him. A horrifying sight met their eyes. As a thick stream of white gas hissed from the pen, the Germans started up in alarm and surprise. The two men asleep died even before they had time to wake up properly, eyes bulging from their sockets, hands grabbing frantically for suddenly burning throats. The earnest private with the rifle tried to get to his feet, but the weapon tumbled from nerveless fingers. Strange, terrible, gurgling noises came from his throat, his mouth opened wide, as he gasped fervently for air until he dropped like a sack of wet cement. Only one of the card players managed to stagger to the glass, trailing cards behind him. For what seemed an age, he stood there crouched like a hunchback, croaking unintelligible pleas for aid, his fingers clawing helplessly at the pane. Abel turned his eyes away in horror and when he looked again, the man was slowly slipping to the floor.

'How long before we can get in there, Mac?' Cain broke the silence, his voice barely under control.

'Give it five more seconds.'

Audibly Cain started to count them off. 'All right,' he commanded when the time was up, 'let's go in there and bed them down on the floor so that they'll look to a casual observer at least, as if they're asleep.'

'Ay, for good,' Mac chuckled. But for once there was no answering laugh from the others; the scene was too terrible, too macabre.

Minutes later they had the dead young men, their faces hideously distorted, their trousers wet where they had urinated in their death throes, bedded down on the floor, their faces buried in their coarse grey blankets.

Grimly Cain closed the door behind him and took a quick look at them. They would fool the casual observer. 'Okay, let's go.'

Kranz knew there was something wrong as

soon as he saw them sprawled out so peacefully under their rough blankets. In his years with the police and later the Gestapo, he had seen a lot of men sleeping in prison cells; young men never slept that peacefully. They tossed and turned in their sleep, plagued by their nocturnal desires and unreasoning fears.

For a moment he stared at them, the same old cigar stump glued to his thick bottom lip. It was three days since he had moved into Fort Driant, and although the General had scorned his suggestion that the trained Tommy killers might attempt to break into the underground fort, he was still uneasy. That was the reason why he was wandering the lonely dark passages now instead of being in the garrison's underground cinema watching that night's attraction, the *Deutsche Wochenschau's* latest newsreel of another National Socialist victory in Russia. For, as he reasoned, if the Tommies did attempt to get into Fort Driant it would be at night.

Sucking a little harder at the cold stump, he opened the door of the glass cage. His nostrils were assailed by the scent of almonds. But it was too pungent for him. He coughed suddenly. 'Asleep on duty, eh?' he called, half hesitant, half alarmed. He applied the toe of his boot to the nearest man. He didn't move.

'Hey,' he said, his voice rising a little. He rammed his boot into the man's ribs, harder this time.

Still the guard did not stir.

'What's the matter with you, soldier?' he demanded harshly in his Gestapo voice. 'Are you drunk or dead-out or something?'

Still the figure swathed in blankets remained silent and immobile.

With a grunt, Kranz bent down. 'I asked you a shitty question!' he rapped and pulled the blanket away from the man. The face revealed was ashen, the bottom lip bitten clean through in agony, the sightless eyes staring up at him in nameless terror. Kranz staggered to his feet. Even before his brain could formulate the words, he knew instinctively that this had to be the work of the Tommy killers. They were already somewhere within the Fort.

The lone sentry crunched slowly past their hiding place, the sound of his boots on the gravelled walk outside the metal door. Mac looked inquiringly at Cain.

Cain shook his head. The sentry was theirs for the taking; he was easy meat with his back to them like that. But Cain told himself there was no need to leave unnecessary clues to their progress behind them.

'Okay, I'll take the lead,' Cain whispered. 'You bring up the rear, Mac.'

'Scots, wha hae!' Mac said, danger forgotten at the prospect of action.

They slipped hastily through the door and began to mount the stairs of the poorly lit HQ buildings, keeping to the edge of the steps where they didn't creak. There was no sound, save the faint chatter of a teleprinter somewhere far down below them. A gloomy corridor stretched away before them. Cain tiptoed carefully to the first leather-covered door. There was a neat precise card fastened to the centre, with the words *Oberstleutnant Dirks, Privat.* He nodded to the others, waiting tensely at the stairs, pistols in hand.

'Yes, these are the private quarters of the senior officers,' he whispered when they had closed on him. 'Come on, let's see if we can find Meyer.'

Like grey timber wolves, they slipped down both sides of the silent, gloomy corridor, searching for their prey, nerves jangling, breath coming suppressed gasps. *'Hauptmann der Panzertruppe Hartmann… Oberst Butz i. GenSt… Major Friderichs…'*

It was Spiv who spotted it. *'General der Luftwaffe Meyer, Privat.* Major, over here – it's him!' Without waiting for them to join him, he bent and placed his ear against the door. There was a faint persistent whirring sound, a few heavy male grunts, punctuated by a girlish giggle, uttered half in embarrassment, half in encouragement. 'He's in there,

Major,' Spiv said straightening up, 'and the fat bugger's at it!' Then almost as an afterthought and to himself. 'I only hope that little randy bitch Marieclair is keeping her knees together.'

Cain pushed Spiv softly to one side and seized the door handle with his steel hook, pistol at the ready in his good hand. Behind him the others tensed. Cain took a deep breath. His claw tightened on the metal door handle. 'All right – *now!*' he hissed and thrust down the handle.

The door swung open, and they were in, tumbling into the glowing, yet darkened room, pistols at the ready, slamming the door shut behind them a fleeting second later.

The Grey Wolf lay stretched out on an enormous bed. Above him a long sun lamp glowed under the ceiling, colouring his massive naked body an unnatural green. Sweat streamed in rivulets from his obscene stomach, while kneeling on either side of him on the rumpled black silk sheets, the naked teenage whores attempted to bring some kind of life to his flaccid organ.

At the sight of the four men they had been awaiting for the last tense thirty minutes, Marieclair and Rosemarie ceased their squeezing and stroking. For what seemed a long time nothing happened. Then like a whale rising from the sea, splattering sweat everywhere, the General lifted himself with ponderous majesty and thrust up his dark leather goggles. He blinked several times, as if he couldn't quite believe what he saw. But there was no fear in his eyes.

Almost cheerfully, he said in a heavy, food-thickened bass, 'So he was right after all.'

Who he was, Cain did not know. Neither did he care. He motioned with his pistol for the girls to get out of the way.

'I hope you haven't been getting your knees that far apart in here,' Spiv called to Marieclair, as he flung Cain the cushion he would need now.

Cain speared it neatly at the end of his gleaming steel hook, while the General watched him as calmly as if he were surveying some mildly interesting military manoeuvre. Swiftly, Cain wrapped the thick, overstuffed cushion around the sawn-off 38, just leaving the muzzle free. He estimated the distance and took a few paces forward.

The Grey Wolf nodded approvingly. 'If you are going to do it, Englishman, make a better job of it than your countrymen did on the Somme in sixteen.' Casually he touched the deep hole gouged in the upper thigh of his pale hairless left leg. The flesh shook obscenely. 'Good for one limp for the last twenty-odd years.'

'I'll try to, General,' Cain replied. Despite his disgust at the man's sweating obscenity, his repulsive attentions to the two teenagers who were now hastily grabbing their clothes together, he could not help but admire the man's bravery.

He raised his pistol, keeping the cushion in place awkwardly with his hook. On the bed, the General's pudgy face tensed, and beneath its sweat-lathered, dimpled grossness, Cain could see the steely battle-hardened soldier of the good years. *General der Luftwaffe* Hans Meyer was going to meet his end bravely like the soldier he had always been. Quite simply he knitted his pudgy hands together to prevent them from trembling too obviously. Cain sucked in his breath and slowly began to squeeze the trigger of his 38.

'*Halt!*' rasped a harsh voice as the door behind Cain was flung open wildly, '*keine Bewegung – oder rich schiesse!*'

With a feeling of near despair, Major Cain let his pistol drop to the floor.

SIX

Kranz hooked his thumb almost casually in the front of Marieclair's black bra and tugged. It ripped open immediately. Her breasts spilled out and she was as naked as she had been five minutes before. The teen-ager's arms flew up to protect her nakedness. Kranz knock them away and with the muzzle of his pistol flipped up each breast to check if anything was hidden beneath the slight droop. There wasn't.

'Must you do that, Kranz?' Meyer asked petulantly, still squatting on the rumpled bed like a green-glowing Buddha, naked under the sun-ray lamp, and not quite recovered from the sudden reversal of his situation.

Kranz puffed at his cigar and knocked the ash on to the General's expensive carpet. 'Yes, General. Those French whores of yours were part of the plot.'

'Those children?'

Kranz nodded and gestured at the four sullen Ultra men lined up against the wall, covered by the half-dressed chauffeur's Schmeisser machine-pistol. 'Those Tommy killers used them to get into here in the first place – oh, yes the little Frog bitches are as bad as they are. Right in it, up to their unwashed necks.'

He turned his attention to Rosemarie, quivering like a leaf, her pale little hands filled with her underwear. He reached out a big hand, his slanting eyes shining at the sight of her fear. He thrust it into the neck of the dress she had managed to fling on to cover her nakedness. His knuckles deliberately grazed her taut, erect nipples. Very slowly, with all his strength, he tore the material downwards, his big thumb tracing a line in the length of her beautiful body, right through the faint puff of pubic hair, and stopping there. She jumped. Kranz grinned evilly and took his thumb away. Slowly he dropped the two halves of flimsy material, his eyes taking in the white gleaming length of her young limbs. Again nothing.

'And are you going to search her too?' the General asked a little angrily, reaching out for a sheet to cover his obscene nudity, but once again very much the general officer.

'No, General. You couldn't hide anything under that pair of peas.' He pointed the wet end of his cigar at Rosemarie's breasts. 'My old mother's pet canaries have better tits than them!'

Oberkommissar Kranz was very pleased with himself at that moment; he had pulled it off again, and this time there would be promotion in it for him. Perhaps 'Gestapo' Muller, his squat, cold-eyed Bavarian boss, would even request his transfer from Aachen back to his native Berlin and Gestapo Headquarters at Number 10 Prinz Albrecht Strasse. In its cellars, with the full range of torture equipment, he could really enjoy himself, and be paid to do so too. Now, complete master of the situation in the General's bedroom, he allowed himself the luxury of savouring his few moments of triumph before removing the crestfallen, sullen Tommy killers.

'You see, General, they came into the Fort in the Horch.'

'My car?'

'Yes, probably in the boot – it's big enough.'

'Could be,' the chauffeur growled, trying to cover up his thirty-minute dalliance with Madame Zaza who had taught him a couple of things about sex in that short time. 'The Madame made me wait. I bet the *Scheisskerle* sneaked into the car then.' He jerked his Schmeisser threateningly at the four Englishmen.

'Anyway,' Kranz frowned at the chauffeur's back for having interfered in his moment of triumph, 'they got in. Then they killed the detachment at Number One Guard Post. Poison gas, I should think.'

'Gas!' Meyer echoed, his vast girth wrapped in a black silk sheet now, so that he looked like a slightly zany Roman emperor.

Kranz nodded. 'It just goes to show what determined, ruthless bastards they really are. As you may remember I warned you.'

'Yes, yes, you don't need to rub it in, Kranz. You warned me – repeatedly.'

'Don't worry, General. We of the *Geheime Staatspolizei* will make them pay back tenfold for the suffering they caused our poor lads out there. By the time we're finished with them,' he gloated, 'they're going to be pleading with us on their knees to be allowed to die.' He puffed happily on his cigar, as if he were already relishing that prospect.

The two naked girls shivered, although they had not understood a word of the German; the look on Kranz's face had sufficed.

'All right, all right,' General Meyer grunted, rising to his feet on the bed, black sheet draped over one glowing shoulder, 'the post-mortem is concluded, I think Kranz. I feel it is time you got them out of here. I've wasted enough time looking a damn fool in here.' He looked sadly at the two little whores, 'And take them with you, too.'

'*Zu Befehl!*' Kranz snapped, remembering his position once again. He waved his Walther at the prisoners. 'All right, you lot, when I give the command, move to that door in single file – and slowly! Albert,' he spoke to the chauffeur, 'don't hesitate to shoot if they make a wrong move–' He grinned suddenly – 'at the kneecap.' He waved his pistol at the two whores. '*Allez, vite, a la borte,*' he ordered in his heavily accented German-French.

The two naked girls, clutching their clothes to their breasts, started to walk fearfully to the door. On the bed, General Meyer sighed, as the delightful little flanks moved out of his life. But still, he consoled himself, in Spain he would undoubtedly find their like.

They had just reached the door when Spiv shouted, 'Marieclair, open yer legs!'

A light dawned in the little whore's eyes. She dropped her clothes, and before Kranz or the chauffeur could react, she spread her boyish thighs and fumbled for something between her legs. With her white teeth bared excitedly, she tossed it between the Ultra men and the chauffeur as Spiv had told her to do if anything went wrong.

It exploded with a surprisingly loud report for such a small device. The chauffeur staggered back, his Schmeisser tilted upwards. An instant later he had recovered himself, but it was too late. Spiv, first off the mark, flung himself at him. He went down with a crash. Spiv's elbow thudded into his chin and as the thick, smoking gas started to steam from the miniature smoke bomb, the machine-pistol tumbled from the chauffeur's nerveless fingers.

Pinching his nostrils together, Cain dived through the smoke. Kranz raised his pistol, coughing thickly already, cigar stump still glued to his bottom lip. Cain's steel hook struck it. Kranz cursed and the gun tumbled from his fingers. With his left hand, he launched a punch at his sudden assailant. Cain ducked and at the same moment, brought up his hook as the Gestapo man stumbled against him, carried forward by

261

his own weight. Kranz ran right on to it. His scream rang out as the cruel steel point penetrated deep into his guts; and he continued to scream as Cain slowly tore the hook up the length of his body.

The others sprang through the cloud of white smoke, coughing and spluttering but unharmed. Cain bent and wiped the blood from the hook on Kranz's tunic; then as an afterthought, removed the glowing cigar from his dead lips and stabbed it out on the General's carpet.

'Gimme the pistol,' he ordered, not taking his gaze off the man standing by the bed. 'The Gestapo man's.'

Abel pushed his way between him and the General, his arms outspread on either side, as if he hoped to cover the German's black-clad bulk with them. 'No,' he said firmly. '*No.*' He pulled a pistol. It was Kranz's. 'There will be no more killing here. We've killed enough.'

Slowly Cain rose to his feet. Time was running out. Someone must have heard the racket. 'Abel,' he said slowly and carefully, while the rest of them watched the two opponents, 'I'm going to kill that man behind you. Get out of my way!'

He took one step forward. Abel's fingers whitened on the butt of the pistol. Cain could read the look in the other man's eyes. Hadn't he seen it often enough in these last terrible years. He stopped in his tracks.

Abel breathed a little sigh of relief. A small nerve had begun to tic at the left side of his hard jaw. 'Thank you, Cain,' he whispered, 'thank you.'

'Well,' Cain demanded icily, 'you've won. What are you going to do?'

Slowly Abel began to lower his pistol, his eyes wary, wondering whether Cain was unscrupulous enough to play a trick on him. Finally he had lowered it to his side; Cain had still not moved from his place.

Abel's face broke into a frank smile. 'Here,' he said. He tossed the pistol at Cain. In his surprise Cain almost dropped it. 'Now look, we've still got to get out of this damned place, haven't we?'

'You're not bloody shitting, Yank!' Spiv said hastily. 'And right bloody smartish too, if you ask me.'

'So, what are we going to do, eh?' Abel asked, still smiling broadly.

The tension broke. On the bed the General heaved an audible sigh of relief, although he had presumably not understood a word of the deadly interchange. The Ultra men and the two teenage whores looked at the American expectantly.

'I'll tell you,' Abel went on. 'We're gonna do this.'

THE GREY SHEEP *(November 1942)*

The Buckinghamshire sky was grey and forbidding as it had been when Major Cain had first driven north towards Bletchley. But this time, despite the dun-coloured sky and the damp November countryside with little pools of fog in the hollows still, there was a strange air of expectancy about everything. He had noted it too in the little towns and villages on his way. For the first time in many a long month, the shabby, war-weary civilians in the streets seemed to have a new light in their eyes, as if they were waiting, eager and tense, for good news.

The Government Code and Cypher School had not changed though. The shabby, tweed-jacketed elderly civilians of the Golf and Chess Club looked just as they had looked three months before: withdrawn, absent. And the Home Guards at the gate were as hard-eyed and suspicious as ever, checking his and the other man's identity twice; going over the staff car as if they expected it to be full of German paras. Finally they allowed them through and Cain turned off before the ornate red-brick house, driving at the regulation five mph towards the rusty Nissen which housed the Ultra unit.

Zero C met him at the door of the hut as soon as the guard had passed him through. He gave the Major one of his hard looks and stretched out his hand. It was as firm as the look in his eyes. 'Glad to see you made it, Cain,' he said, his voice unemotional. 'Tempsford telephoned me as soon as they picked you up last night.'

'Thank you. I came up as soon as I could pick up a car and get my chaps settled. They've had a bad time of it these last few weeks.'

Zero C wasn't interested. Without even offering the one-handed Major, face drawn and pale from the weeks of hiding, a chair, he said accusingly. 'Well, Ultra didn't pull it off after all, eh?'

'I wouldn't say that, exactly,' Cain replied carefully.

Zero C looked at him sharply. 'What do you mean – exactly.'

'Well, I don't suppose you've heard anything of the Grey Wolf these last few weeks, have you?' Cain asked.

'No, that is true. He moved his HQ to Lorraine, you know.'

Cain nodded.

'And after that, we heard nothing. Not even the usual routine traffic.' He looked at Cain in sudden suspicion. 'What's going on, Cain?'

But before Cain could answer, an inner door opened to admit a wing commander around forty with greying hair and bright blue eyes. His keen face was full of restrained excitement. Impatiently he flung an inquiring look at Zero C. The civilian nodded.

'It's all right, Humph, he's in on this.'

'Good.' As businesslike as the high-pressure salesman he had once been, he thrust an Ultra intercept at Zero C. 'Just in. It's from the German Resident in North Africa to the *OKW.* He reports our boys have just started landing there.'

Zero C's thin, cold face lit up. 'Oh, I say,' he exclaimed, 'what wonderful news! Torch is going in!' Then his look of restrained joy disappeared. 'And ... the Hun reaction?'

'Predictably the OKW has ordered an immediate occupation of the unoccupied part of France.' Humph tugged at the end of his sharp nose. 'Vichy's had it.'

'And, er Meyer – the Spanish business, Humph?'

The Wing Commander shook his greying head. 'Nothing, absolute silence. Not a sausage, Zero C.'

Zero C sighed with relief. 'Thank God for that!'

'I don't think you quite heard me,' Cain said softly, after the Wing Commander had disappeared briskly into the inner office. 'I wonder if you would mind coming outside with me for a moment? I'd like to introduce you to someone.'

'Oh, all right,' Zero C said impatiently. 'Lead on man, if you must.'

They walked outside into the raw November morning. A strange sight met Zero C's eyes there. A civilian was handcuffed to the wheel of the Humber staff car which Cain had borrowed from 138th Squadron's Motor Pool. He was wearing the same shabby suit he had been wearing ever since they had taken his glittering uniform from him, after he had safely extracted them from Fort Driant as Abel had suggested he might be so kind as to do. With a loaded pistol stuck in the small of his back, they had driven through the guards goggling open-mouthed at the two naked girls cuddling up to him. In spite of the poor quality French suit and the fact that it hung in folds on a body shrunk to a shadow of its former self by the privations of the last terrible weeks on the run, there was no denying the man's military bearing.

'Who is this man?' Zero asked, as the strange handcuffed civilian glowered at him angrily. 'Well?' he demanded, the truth beginning to dawn on him. 'Do you mean Ultra pulled it off after all?'

Cain nodded. 'Right in one... May I introduce you to *General der Luftwaffe* Hans

Meyer, once known as the Grey Wolf, though,' he added as an afterthought, 'the way he looks at this moment, it might be more opportune to call him the Grey Sheep, don't you think?'

This Large Print Book, for people
who cannot read normal print,
is published under the auspices of

THE ULVERSCROFT FOUNDATION